'Freddy ju  **lp on his belt**

'He only pick ... say no. He thinks I'm a challenge.'

'I would have said that's not true,' Dan said after a moment's reflection. 'I think he has a genuine...regard for you.'

Sue had thought this too. But it was no good, even if Freddy was sincere. She decided she had to fight back. 'Do you always take such an interest in the love lives of your staff?'

Once again Dan seemed unmoved by her apparent annoyance. 'I take an interest in all my staff,' he said, 'and at Freddy's age that often means taking an interest in their love lives.'

'Well, I haven't got a love life, and I don't want or need one!'

Gill Sanderson is a psychologist who finds time to write only by staying up late at night. Weekends are filled by her hobbies of gardening, running and mountain walking. Her ideas come from her work, from one son who is an oncologist, one son who is a nurse and her daughter who is a trainee midwife. She first wrote articles for learned journals and chapters for a textbook. Then she was encouraged to change to fiction by her husband, who is an established writer of war stories.

Recent titles by the same author:

A SON FOR JOHN
SEVENTH DAUGHTER

A MAN TO BE TRUSTED

BY
GILL SANDERSON

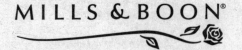

MILLS & BOON®

*All the characters in this book have no existence outside the imagination
of the author, and have no relation whatsoever to anyone bearing the
same name or names. They are not even distantly inspired by any
individual known or unknown to the author, and all the incidents are
pure invention.*

*First published in Great Britain 2000
Harlequin Mills & Boon Limited,
Eton House, 18-24 Paradise Road, Richmond, Surrey TW9 1SR*

© Gill Sanderson 2000

ISBN 0 263 82254 0

*Set in Times Roman 10½ on 12 pt.
03-0008-50563*

*Printed and bound in Spain
by Litografia Rosés, S.A., Barcelona*

CHAPTER ONE

'I ASKED to work nights,' Sue McCain explained. 'I don't have a complicated social life and I'm happy to help out those with families and so on.'

Sister Reeves, the new shift leader, dubiously surveyed the slim figure in front of her. Midwife McCain had only just qualified, and wore new navy-blue tunic and trousers instead of the whites of the student. No make-up, short black hair, no attempt to make herself stand out. But Sister Reeves knew that the heart-shaped face and brown eyes had turned many heads at Emmy's—Emmeline Penistone's Women's Hospital. And Sue had paid no attention at all.

'A young girl like you should be out, enjoying yourself, not having to sleep all day,' Sister suggested.

'I'm twenty-five and I enjoy being a midwife. I've just qualified, there's such a lot more I want to learn and the night shift is the best time for that. Come on, Sister, aren't you pleased to see a bit of enthusiasm?'

When Sue smiled Sister knew at once why men were attracted to her. Her face seemed to come alive.

'I always like enthusiasm. And I see you're on a seven day rotation. You can get about a bit in the week you have off.'

'No chance, I need the time to study. I'm happy in my work, Sister. I spent enough time gadding about when I was younger.'

Sister shook her head, mock-mournfully. 'So did I. It's terrible when you get old. You know, when you

5

turn twenty-one. Come on, I'll introduce you to the
rest of the night shift.'

In fact, Sue already knew most of the midwives
grouped waiting for handover. She had done most of
her practical training at Emmy's and had leapt at the
chance of a job when it had been offered to her.
Emmy's had a national, if not an international reputation, and Sue had known it was a good place to start
her career. She grabbed herself a plastic cup of coffee
from the machine in the corner and said hello to those
that she knew.

Quickly she glanced at the whiteboard that indicated
the name and condition of every woman in labour.
There were only seven patients, six in low-dependency
rooms and one in a high-dependency room. Not a
lot—it could be a quiet shift. But, then, in Maternity,
anything could happen.

She looked at the details of the patient in the high
dependency room. Forty weeks pregnant, being looked
after by midwife Jo Colls, SROM. Membranes had
ruptured spontaneously, five centimetres dilated, dia-
morphine—an opiate—had been administered once.
She shuddered slightly as she saw the cryptic note
'G5P2'. It told her that the mother had been pregnant
five times, had two living children and one about to
be born. Two miscarriages. However, that patient
wouldn't be hers—a more experienced midwife was
in charge.

She was allocated Jenny Doyle in room five. Sue
smiled at Stella Robinson, the midwife in charge so
far. Stella had sometimes supervised her while she'd
been training. 'She's sound,' Sister Reeves had said.
That had been high praise and Sue and Stella had got
to be firm friends.

'Hi, Sue,' Stella said, yawning. 'Think you've got an easy one tonight. In fact, she's only just come in— I haven't finished examining her yet. Brought herself in by taxi.'

'Brought herself in? No partner, no mother, no friend?' It was very unusual for someone to come in on her own. Although partners or mums could be a problem during labour—the men much more than the women—in general, Sue liked having a relation in. It calmed the mother and certainly helped bonding.

'Nobody with her. Jenny Doyle seems to be a bit of a loner. No wedding ring or sign of a partner. She's very quiet and self-possessed. She's a primigravida but doesn't seem at all worried.'

'All sorts of women have babies.' Sue remembered a much-quoted line from one of her tutors. 'And every birth is different, as well as being the same.'

'Is she still coming out with that old chestnut? I remember her telling us that twenty years ago. Mind you, she's right. Now…' Stella had time for a joke, but handover was a serious business and every midwife was at pains to get things right. She handed Sue a folder. 'Here's the early labour record. Like I said, she's only been with me for ten minutes so I haven't finished checking her yet. She's on the monitor. Contractions every three minutes, strong on palpations, looks like she's doing something.'

'Looks like she's doing something'—midwife-ese for it looked like the baby was coming.

'Sounds straightforward. Lead me to her.' The two set off down the corridor.

'One other thing,' Stella said, half-hopefully. 'A week on Friday we're having a bit of a farewell bash for Merry Stirling. She's been a midwife for twelve years, and she's leaving to have her first baby. She ought to have more sense! Anyway, most of the obs and gynae staff are coming, as well as a lot of the rest of the hospital. We've hired the hospital social club, and there'll be a presentation and a disco. Why don't you come? Let your hair down a bit?'

Sue could tell by her tone that Stella guessed what Sue's answer would be. 'I'm sorry, Stella, it's just not my sort of thing. I'll give something if you're making a collection and I'd like to come to the presentation. But discos just aren't my style.'

Stella grinned ruefully. 'Well, I tried,' she said. 'I can honestly tell him I tried.'

'Him?' Sue winked at her friend. 'Don't tell me, let me guess—you're running errands for young Dr Freddy Sharp.'

'You've discovered my guilty secret. Freddy loves you from a distance, and a distance is what you keep him at. Seriously, Sue, he's not all that bad. Why don't you come along with him?'

'I've no time for men friends, I have to think of my career,' Sue said flippantly. 'Now, it's time to work.'

They walked in together. It still gave Sue a little thrill to enter a room where shortly a baby was to be born, to see the apprehensive or joyful mother, the cot waiting with folded blankets, tiny nightgown and nappy. Around the walls were the suction tube, oxygen mask, air and gas mask and all the other aids that modern medicine had developed. But most of the time giving birth was something that a woman did herself, and, as midwife, Sue felt privileged to help her.

'I'm going now, Jenny,' Stella said to the heavily breathing figure under the white sheet. 'But I'm leav-

ing you in the more than competent hands of Sue
McCain here. I'm sure you'll have a lovely baby.'

'Thanks, Stella.' She gasped in reply. 'Ow! Nobody
told me it would feel like this.'

Sue moved forward as Stella quietly slipped out.
'Would you like some gas and air to ease the pain a
bit, Jenny?' she asked. 'We have it here.'

Jenny shook her head, the sweat glistening on her
face as she did so. 'I'm all right,' she said through
gritted teeth. 'At least, for now I'm all right.'

'Is there anyone we should tell you're in here?' Sue
asked delicately. 'Your partner or a family member?'

'No. I'm an academic, I'm getting older and I
wanted a baby but not a partner. The biological father
of my child will have nothing to do with it.'

'If that's your decision,' Sue said. It wasn't her
place to judge.

She reached for a cloth and gently wiped the hot
brow. 'I'm just going to check the monitor to see that
the baby's heartbeat is OK,' she said. 'And I'll check
your contractions, too. Then I'll do the baseline observations—temperature, pulse and blood pressure.
Just making sure you're healthy.' It was important always—or nearly always—to tell the mother what you
were doing. After all, she was the one giving birth.

All the observations were fine so far. Next, Sue
gently palpated the top of Jenny's abdomen. The fun-
dus, the top of the womb, was at the right height. Sue
moved her hands down and felt for the baby's head.
She frowned. She could feel all of the head, it was
mobile. It wasn't engaged, not sitting in the arch of
the pelvis. Normally, in a primigravida, the head engaged between thirty-six and thirty-eight weeks. This
was not serious but definitely a cause for concern.

'Your waters haven't broken yet, have they?' Sue asked, trying to sound casual.

'Not yet. I wish they would. I want to get on with this.'

'I'm afraid you might be quite a while yet. Now, try to relax, I'm slipping out for a minute. If you need help, just press this here.' She showed Jenny the little plastic buzzer hanging by the side of the bed.

Taking Jenny's notes, Sue went in search of the shift leader. This was something she had to hand on.

'Why didn't the community midwife diagnose this earlier?' Sister Reeves grumbled, leafing through the notes. 'Oh, I see. Our Jenny Doyle has been too busy to see her midwife for the past three weeks. She could have saved us all some trouble—and perhaps made things easier for herself.'

'I'll go and find Freddy,' Sue said. Behind her, Sister wrote 'SHO' by the side of Jenny Doyle's name on the whiteboard. He was now in charge.

Sue found Freddy Sharp, the senior house officer, sprawled in the sister's room, his long legs propped up on the waste-paper basket. He was deep in consideration of the sporting pages of the evening paper. 'Susan McCain, my favourite midwife,' he said as she entered. 'I knew it. You couldn't resist me any longer and you've come along to tell me that you will go with me to Merry Stirling's ball. Together we can—'

'We've got a problem in room five,' Sue interrupted. 'Forty weeks gone, she's in labour and the head hasn't engaged.'

Freddy knew when to be serious. He stood, refastened his tie and pulled the edges of his white coat together. 'Ah. Waters broken yet?'

'Not yet. Things otherwise seem to be going quite smoothly, but…'

'Let's go to have a look.'

Sue had to admit that Freddy was developing quite a good bedside manner. He introduced himself to Jenny, chatted for a moment and explained that there was always a doctor hanging around somewhere, and this evening he was it. Then he looked through Jenny's notes, checked the monitor and lastly gently palpated her abdomen himself. He smiled at Jenny and left, beckoning Sue to follow him.

Outside the door he went up further in Sue's estimation. 'I think the decision is beyond me,' he said honestly. 'I want the senior registrar to look at her.'

'Are you going to send home for him?'

'It's not necessary. I saw him on one of the wards an hour ago. I'll bleep him.'

'Who is it?' Sue asked curiously. 'The only one I've ever had dealings with was Dr Rumney.' She didn't say that she had found Dr Rumney a doctor of the old school, firmly convinced that his position was next to that of God, and that nurses, midwives and junior doctors were there to observe, admire and say nothing.

'It's not Rumney, thank goodness. Dan Webster's much more approachable—you can learn from him. Now, you sit with Jenny and I'll see if I can get him.'

'Just what is going on?' Jenny asked when Sue reentered the room. 'If there's something wrong then I want to know.' Sue could tell that Jenny was trying to be in control, trying to deal with any problem in a reasoned manner. But she was having a baby and her body and her emotions were betraying her.

Sue took her hand, and felt the fear in the tightness of the grip. 'Just a minor problem,' she said quietly.

'To be on the safe side, we've sent for the senior man here. We're probably worrying you and making a lot of fuss over nothing, but since he's handy we thought we'd have him over.'

'I'm frightened, Sue.'

'There's no need to be. Just try to relax. You'll feel a lot better when you've talked to Dr Webster.'

In fact, everyone felt a lot better when Dan Webster walked in. Sue could tell at once why everyone found him reassuring. He was big. Big shoulders, big arms, a big chest. By comparison, Freddy was skinny. But Dan's size wasn't threatening. His face was pleasantly rough-hewn and remarkably attractive. When he smiled you knew that he was your friend, and you wanted to be his friend, too.

He winked at Sue, but said nothing to her. Instead, he moved straight to Jenny's bedside and smiled down at her. 'I've always regretted being a man,' he told her dolefully, 'because when I tell a pregnant young lady like you that I know how she feels, she promptly replies, "Oh, no, you don't." And, of course, she's right. But I love helping ladies have babies, and I want to help you.'

Sue could see Jenny relaxing as she listened to this. She knew it was nonsense but she liked it. 'I'm Jenny Doyle,' she said, offering a hand. 'Actually, Doctor, but not a doctor of medicine.'

'Fantastic! You're a doctor of…?'

'I'm a linguist, I study—Ow!' Jenny's face twisted as a contraction, harder than usual, hit her.

'I think we'll leave the intellectual discussion till later,' Dan said. 'Now, the problem is Jenny, that your baby hasn't come down far enough—its head isn't engaged. This is unusual but not too worrying yet. What we'll do first is fetch a portable scanner and have a look at baby. You just relax, and we'll fetch the wonder machine from next door.'

The scanner was always on hand. Sue fetched it, and she, Freddy and Dan clustered round the monitor and watched the squirming black and white lines on the screen.

'Head's high, but otherwise everything is fine.' Dan said with satisfaction. 'Look Jenny, that's your baby wriggling.'

He turned the screen and Jenny craned her neck to see. 'Now, just lie back and relax,' Dan went on, 'I'm going to give you another internal and then we'll have a little confabulation and decide what to do.'

Jenny did relax as Sue held back the sheet and Dan conducted a swift and deft examination. 'Good, good,' he said. 'Four centimetres dilated. Everything doing nicely.' He indicated that Freddy and Sue were to follow him out of the room.

Outside the door Sue found a large hand thrust at her. 'Nice to meet you, Sue,' Dan said genially. 'Welcome to the team. And especially, congratulations on the exam results.'

She looked at him, nonplussed both by his comment and by the unexpected frisson when they'd touched. She tried to be practical. 'Exam results?'

'You got a first in your midwifery degree. That takes some doing and I'm happy to be working with someone who is that bright.'

'How did you know I got a first?'

'I like to know about people I work with, know what they are capable of, so I looked you up. Now, Jenny in there, what d'you think we should do?'

'I've only read about it, never seen a case,' Sue said

honestly. 'But since there's a chance of cord prolapse, perhaps she should have an ARM— an artificial rupture of the membranes. That would move things along a bit.'

'I see. Freddy?'

'I agree entirely. And I've only ever seen one before.'

'Good. Fortunately, that's what I think is best, so let's go and tell Jenny.'

She was very aware of Dan's long look at her before they returned to the room.

While they had been out Jenny had started worrying again. She turned a panic-stricken face to the little group. 'What's the matter with me?' she demanded. 'What are you going to do next?'

Dan sat by her side and stroked her arm comfortingly. 'Your baby's head isn't quite far enough down for this stage of the birth,' he explained comfortingly. 'There's no need to worry too much, but the risk is that the cord that attaches the baby to your placenta might get trapped—and that would cut off the baby's supply of oxygen and nourishment. So Sue here is going to ease your baby's head to the proper position, and I'm going to break your waters. We'll do it in Theatre but you won't need anaesthetic or anything.'

'Thank you, Doctor.' Jenny gasped. 'I like it when...when you explain things.'

'All part of the service. Now, I'm going to sort out a theatre—we should be with you in a couple of minutes.'

Dan and Freddy left, and Sue took Dan's place by the side of the bed. 'He's a nice man, isn't he?' Jenny said. 'Do you—Oof!'

It started off as a contraction, but Sue knew instantly what had happened. Jenny's waters had broken. She threw back the covers and reached automatically for the box of sterile gloves. 'Don't worry,' Sue said, snapping them round her wrists. 'Now there'll be no need to…' A thrill of horror shook her. There, protruding, was a section of pulsating, pink-purple cord.

No time to panic! With her elbow she smacked the emergency buzzer. Ignoring Jenny's cries of alarm, she inserted two fingers and carefully eased the cord back inside, away from the air that would dry it. Then she felt for the baby's head and delicately moved it away from the cord. The cord was still pulsating, feeding the baby. It couldn't be allowed to stop!

The door behind her crashed open, and suddenly the room was full of people—Freddy, Dan, Sister Reeves, two more midwives. Sister Reeves took in the situation at once and moved to Jenny's side to take her hand and try to calm her. Sue made a quick report. 'Jenny's waters broke, the cord prolapsed. I eased it back inside and I'm holding the head away from it.'

Miraculously, Dan's voice was still calm. 'Well done, Sue. Now, whatever happens, keep that head and cord separate. It's not worth the risk to try to remove your hand—just concentrate on that and ignore us. OK?'

'I can do it.'

'Freddy, crash bleep, we've got an emergency section. I want to operate in five minutes. Round up an anaesthetist and a pediatrician.'

Still calm, he turned and smiled at Jenny. 'Baby's in a bit of a hurry, Jenny. We're going to have to give you an emergency Caesarean section. But don't worry, we've got a good team here and we're on top of everything so far. Sister here will give you a form to sign, there'll be a drink of medicine, which won't taste too bad, and one of the midwives will give you a partial shave.'

'What about Sue? What's Sue doing to me?'

'Sue's making sure that baby's all right till we get you into Theatre. She's doing a good job. Now, I know it's an impossible thing to ask, but try to relax if you can. I'll see you in Theatre in a couple of minutes. Keep smiling!'

'I haven't even started smiling yet,' Jenny forced out, and Sue felt more confident. It wasn't much of a joke, but if Jenny could try then she was a fighter. If they could get the baby out before the cord got caught, if she could keep the face away from the cord, then there would be a happy ending. Too many ifs. This wasn't like the easy births she'd been accustomed to so far.

Sister Reeves was now in charge in the room, preparing Jenny for the emergency operation. First she got a scrawl on the operation consent form—there were always some handy. Then Jenny was given a strong antacid to prevent her aspirating her own vomit when anaesthetized. As a midwife quickly shaved the section of Jenny's abdomen where the incision would come, Sister ran through the rest of the check list— the last time Jenny had eaten or drunk, whether she had any allergies; removal of anything loose in the mouth, jewels, contact lenses, hearing aids. Jenny's red nail varnish was removed with acetone—a surgeon might need to check the lips and nails for the tell-tale blue tinge that suggested cyanosis.

And all this time Sue stood, her entire consciousness concentrated on the tops of her two fingers. The cord and the baby's head were still apart. She could feel the cord pulsating. It mustn't stop!

The phone rang—they were ready in Theatre. 'Keep your fingers where they are,' Sister ordered Sue. 'Climb carefully onto the bed and kneel astride Jenny. It doesn't matter what it looks like—you're doing a necessary job.'

Sue did as she was told. A cloth was thrown lightly over Jenny's abdomen and Sue's wrist, and then the entire team pushed the bed rapidly down the corridor to the theatre anteroom. Carefully, her hand still in place, Sue climbed off and many hands lifted Jenny gently onto the theatre cot. Someone pulled a cap onto Sue's head and draped a sterile green gown round her. The anaesthetist placed a mask over Jenny's face, and when she was unconscious deftly intubated her. The cot was pushed into Theatre. Sue's hand was still in place.

Dan was waiting, already gowned and masked. Sue couldn't see his mouth because of the mask, but she saw the corners of his eyes crinkle and knew he was smiling. 'We've all done a good job so far,' he said, 'and I'm looking forward to a happy ending. Sue, keep your fingers where they are till I tell you to move them.' He leaned forward and made a swift incision.

Sue had seen Caesarean sections before, of course, so she could appreciate Dan's skill. He was moving fast, but not so fast as to endanger his patient. After a while she could feel the knife cutting towards her fingers, an eerie sensation.

'You can take your hand away now, Sue.' Dan was lifting the slippery little bundle out, and as he handed it to the extra midwife they all heard the first tentative cry. 'It's a little girl,' the midwife said.

Sue couldn't tell how, but the atmosphere in the theatre changed. No one said anything or smiled, but there was a feeling of relaxation, of happiness. She went to clean herself up, now that the baby was the paediatrician's concern. The midwife handed the baby over and the paediatrician checked her carefully. A minute later he spoke. 'This baby is fine. You don't need me any more.'

Dan looked up from his suturing and nodded. 'Thanks, Chris. See you later perhaps.' Then he looked at Sue who had returned. 'Still your baby, Sue. D'you want to finish off?'

'I certainly do. I've got an interest in this one.'

She took the now steadily wailing bundle into the recovery room, wrapped her up and weighed her. Then she wrote up her notes for the partogram, the semi-legal document that detailed everything about the baby's birth. She slipped the all important three bands onto the baby, two pink rather than the blue for a boy, one white. On the bands were written the mother's name and the unit number.

Ten minutes later Jenny was wheeled into the recovery room. 'You've got a perfect little girl,' Sue whispered to her, and for a moment laid the baby on her breast. There was a quick flicker of delight, and then Jenny's eyes closed again.

Mother and baby were now no longer in Sue's care. They would be taken to the maternity base ward and looked after by a different team. Often Sue felt that she would have liked to have been part of the entire process—getting to know a mother, taking part in the antenatal care, the birth and then the postnatal follow-up. But that wasn't the way hospitals were organised. Her place was on the delivery suite. Still, she'd manage some time the next day to go and see Jenny and her new child.

'An exciting hour,' Sister Reeves said to her. 'There's nothing for you at the moment so why don't you go for a coffee-break?'

'I think I need one,' Sue agreed.

There was only Freddy in the coffee-room when she got there. He'd just poured himself a drink and he poured her one, too. 'Interesting evening,' he greeted her. 'I think I learned a lot, but I wouldn't want to go through that every night.'

She quite liked Freddy. When he stuck to talking professionally, she thought they got on quite well. 'My first ever prolapse,' she agreed.

'I've read about them, of course, and I've seen pictures, but to have to deal with one in real life—it was something else. Wasn't Dan Webster good?'

'You've not met him before?' Freddy seemed surprised when Sue shook her head. 'He's a live wire. Don't let that relaxed appearance fool you—it's only to calm the patients. He's always doing something. He'll listen to anyone, cleaner or consultant, and he's never too busy to help you out. As well as being Specialist Reg, he's organising the hospital fund-raising committee, and if that's not a thankless job I don't know what is. But he does it, and he does it well. He says you should always ask a busy man to do a job.'

Sue was quite surprised at Freddy's enthusiasm. He was usually far too laid back to enthuse about anyone or anything. Dan Webster had to be someone special. 'I'm looking forward to working with him,' she said. 'When I was training I knew he was here—but I've never met him.'

Freddy sipped his coffee and then said, apparently

casually, 'He's had a hand in organising Merry Stirling's farewell do a week next Friday. He's going to make a speech. If you came with me we could probably share a table with him. Why don't we—'

'No, Freddy. I'm not going there with you, I'm not going out with you, I'm not going out with anybody. Why d'you keep on asking me? I've told you no at least once a month for the past year.'

'A constant drip will wear away a stone?' he suggested.

'A constant drip is just a constant drip. Irritating. There are lots of other nurses or midwives who would go out with you—why don't you ask them?'

'Because I fancy you. Don't you fancy me at all?'

She sighed. Why did she have to go through this so frequently? 'No, Freddy, I don't. I like you and I think we work well together, but that's all. I wish just once you'd recognise that I don't want to go out with you— I don't want to go out with anyone. I'm happy in my work and I don't need your idea of a social life. Isn't that clear?'

Dealing with Jenny's prolapsed cord, it had given Sue an adrenaline high and her judgement was slightly at fault. Previously when he had asked her out she had always managed to keep Freddy calm but this time she had annoyed him.

'You can't be a recluse all your life!'

'I'm not a recluse, Freddy. I just want to—'

'I suppose you two lovebirds have drunk all the coffee?' The voice was calm but it took them both by surprise. In the doorway was Dan, now out of his greens, smiling apparently amiably at the pair of them.

'We're not lovebirds,' Sue snapped.

'It seems not. But I still need coffee. I do hope there's some left.'

'There's plenty,' said Freddy quickly, and poured a cup. 'Biscuit?'

Dan took the coffee. Sue noted that he took it strong and black, but with sugar in it—the drink of a man who spent long hours without sleep. 'I feel like treating myself,' Dan announced. 'I think I'll have two biscuits.'

He sat and looked at Sue, half amiably, half quizzically. She saw that his eyes were brown, and she looked away from the steadiness of his gaze. This man disturbed her in a way that Freddy could never manage.

'Quite exciting, that prolapse,' Dan said. 'Since I was busy at the time I didn't have chance to say it, but you did well in there Midwife McCain. It all had a happy ending but that was down to you. If you hadn't acted so quickly, things would have been different. Congratulations.'

Sue felt ridiculously pleased with his praise. 'It was my job,' she said, 'but I must admit I was a bit frightened.'

'Good. You're too young to be over-confident. It's good to be frightened on occasion.'

She didn't believe he was ever frightened. Somehow Dan radiated confidence. She had seen it calming Jenny, knew it would affect all his patients. It was even affecting her now!

Dan turned to Freddy. 'I think we might have a problem in the high dependency room. I want you to go there now, have a look at the lady and then drop in there every hour or so. I'm going to get some sleep—there's a spare bed in the anxious dads' section. But any query at all, you're to wake me.'

'I'm on my way,' Freddy said. 'See you, Sue. Think about Merry Stirling's farewell do—it should be good.' He put down his cup and strode out.

'There's no real need for Freddy to look in on the high dependency case,' Sue said. 'Mary Hall is a very experienced midwife, and she knows when to call for help.'

'I know,' Dan said comfortably. 'But being asked to do something makes him feel loved and wanted, and he looks up to me because of my high position.'

Sue had to giggle. 'You're a manipulator. Would you treat me the same way?'

'Certainly not. I wouldn't get away with it. You're ten years older than Freddy.'

'I am not! I'm only twenty-five.'

'That's in one kind of years. In another kind of years you are far older. You've…experienced far more than Freddy.'

How did he know that? This man was far too bright, far too discerning. She would have to be careful with him. She decided to take refuge in silence and didn't reply to his remark. But he seemed unfazed by her quietness.

'Do I understand that you're thinking of not going to Merry Stirling's farewell party?' he asked after a while. 'I'm organising it. I shall take your non-appearance as a personal slight.'

Sue smiled thinly. 'I shall go to the presentation,' she said, 'so you won't need to feel insulted. But I won't be going with Freddy.'

'Why not? Fine upstanding young consultant-to-be. In time he'll be good. And I can tell he likes you.'

'Freddy just wants another scalp on his belt,' Sue said tartly. 'There's a dozen attractive nurses, young doctors or midwives who would be only too glad to go out with him. He only picks on me because I always say no. He thinks I'm a challenge.'

'I would have said that's not true,' Dan said after a moment's reflection. 'I think he has a genuine...regard for you.'

Sue had thought this, too. But it was no good, even if he was sincere. For a start Freddy *was* far too young for her, even if they were approximately the same age.

She decided she had to fight back. 'Do you always take such an interest in the love lives of your staff?'

Once again he seemed unmoved by her apparent annoyance. 'I take an interest in all my staff,' he said, 'and at Freddy's age that often means taking an interest in their love lives.'

'Well, I haven't got a love life, and I don't want or need one!'

'Ah! The mystery of the barking dog, Holmes.'

She looked at him, perplexed. 'The mystery of the what?'

'It's a famous Sherlock Holmes remark. In one of his stories, a guard dog didn't bark. The mystery was, why not? I think it's mysterious that you don't have, want or need a love life. Still, I'm rambling on. You need to get back to work and I need to get some sleep.'

They both stood, placing their empty cups on the counter. 'To work!' he said, and wrapped an arm round her shoulder. It was, she knew, only a friendly gesture. But she couldn't help herself. She flinched.

She knew he'd noticed it, and after a moment he

removed his arm. Those shrewd brown eyes locked onto hers, but he said nothing. 'See you around, Sue,' he said, and strolled out of the door. She sighed. It had been an eventful few hours.

CHAPTER TWO

AFTER that it was largely a quiet night. Twice Sue was buzzed to go and help another midwife—to take the baby. There were always two midwives present at the moment of birth.

The first time was simple, as it should have been, only taking fifteen or twenty minutes. When the baby's anterior shoulder was showing, Sue injected one mil of syntometrine into the mother's thigh. Then, moments later, she took the baby, did the initial check, slipped on a nappy, wrapped the baby and handed the now wailing little bundle to the ecstatic mother. She tidied up, wrote up the baby notes and slipped on the three bands. Then she walked out. Simple and straightforward.

The second time was slightly more complicated—a human problem, not a natal one. Sue was buzzed slightly before she would have expected. She was introduced to the mother and then the midwife went on, 'And that is Mr Walsh in the corner.' Sue could tell by the tone of her voice that the midwife thought that the husband was—or could be—a problem.

He was not, as expected, by the bedside, holding his wife's hand. Instead, he was sitting in the far corner of the room by a half opened window. Sue could feel a gentle draught.

'I'm not used to this,' he muttered to Sue as she went over to speak to him. 'I just felt a bit sick, so I thought I'd get a bit of fresh air.'

There was a groan from his wife and he bent over, clutching his stomach. Sue could smell the alcohol on his breath—it was hard not to. Mr Walsh had apparently had more than a little to drink. Glancing over her shoulder, Sue saw that it would be a few minutes before she was needed.

Slipping a hand under his shoulder, she pulled him upright. 'Why don't you walk down the corridor, get a bit more fresh air,' she suggested. 'There's a cloak-room down there—you could wash your face.'

She half dragged, half eased the man out of the room, ignoring the plaintive cry from the soon-to-be mother. 'John!'

'She wants me there,' John mumbled outside. 'Got to be with my wife.'

'You'll not help at all if you faint or are sick all over her,' Sue said sharply. 'Now, wash your face, and come back in when you feel better.' They had been told that fathers-to-be reacted in different ways, but she still had difficulty in hiding her feelings. At a time like this a woman needed her husband. The least he could do was stay sober!

In fact, the birth was straightforward, and the pale-faced husband managed to come back in to greet his new son. Sue thought he seemed pleased enough with him. It wasn't her place to judge, she reminded herself.

After that things were quite straightforward, and it was a quiet night. She chatted with the other mid-wives, found a quiet corner and studied a little. There was still so much to learn.

One of the minor pleasures of working nights was the drive home in the morning. After the warmth, and that faint, all-pervasive hospital odour, it was good to feel the freshness of the September sun and smell the grass that had just been cut in the neighbouring park. It was too good a morning to go to bed! As usual, she would enjoy herself for a couple of hours.

As she drove home she thought about Dan Webster. She was rather looking forward to seeing more of the man, even if she did find him disturbing and he paid closer attention to her than she found comfortable. She thought she could learn from him. He seemed to be a doctor who believed in involving all of those around him—not like some others she had dealt with!

Home for Sue was a large semi-detached house in a district called Challis, about five miles from the hospital. Once Challis had been a village, but the town had expanded and flowed round it. However, there was still a village atmosphere to Challis, and Sue liked the area.

She parked her Escort next to the other two cars belonging to the girls she shared the house with—Jane Cabot, a theatre scrub nurse, and Megan Taylor, a senior house officer. They all worked at Emmy's, and got on well together.

The other two were having breakfast together. Sue shouted hello, then went upstairs to change out of the tracksuit she'd picked to travel in and into scruffy shorts, T-shirt and boots. Then she went downstairs to share a cup of tea with the other two before they set off for work.

The three of them got on well together—probably because they didn't try to interfere in each other's lives. Only occasionally would they all manage to have a meal together. They had worked out a set of rules that enabled them to live in harmony, and they stuck to them. The first rule was simple—if you dirty a pot, you wash it. There was never any washing-up left.

There was time for a quick five-minute conversation—Megan especially was interested in the story of the prolapse—and then Sue was left alone. She smiled as she heard the two cars accelerate into the road. She liked her two friends—but she'd been with people all night. She wanted some solitude.

At the back of the house there was a large garden. As ever, when she went out to look at it, she was filled with a sense of peace, of achievement. This was her garden. Over the past four years she had turned it from a wilderness into a little haven where she could escape from the world. Most of her leisure hours were spent here. She surveyed the greenhouse, the neat vegetable plot, the cunningly designed borders and rockery, and felt her heart swell with pride. She had created something.

But gardens need constant attention. She fetched tools from the shed at the bottom of the garden and started to dead-head her roses.

Some time later a voice behind her said, 'I was told I'd find you here. What a wonderful garden.'

She recognised the voice at once, though she'd only heard it for the first time a few hours before. It was friendly, enthusiastic. What in heaven's name had brought Dan Webster to her vegetable patch while she was digging up her potatoes?

She turned. He was standing on her lawn, dressed casually in chinos and a white T-shirt. She noticed the size of his shoulders and the trimness of his waist—there wasn't an ounce of fat on him. He looked cool, neat and clean, and she was aware that she was hot, sticky and almost certainly had dirt stains on her face.

'What are you doing here?' she asked aggressively. She felt at a disadvantage—she would have preferred to have met him when she was cool and groomed herself.

Perceptively, he realised this. 'I came to see you,' he said, 'and now you're angry at me for bursting in on you uninvited. And you're working, too. Why don't you relax a minute and I'll finish digging up these potatoes?' Before she knew what he was doing he had taken the fork from her.

'You can't dig in clothes like that,' she said. 'You'll ruin your trousers and T-shirt.'

'If they get dirty then they'll wash,' he said calmly, sticking the fork into the ground and carefully shaking off the earth. He peered at the potatoes. 'You've got a good crop here. These are interesting— what are they? Pink Fir?'

He was using the fork with what she recognised as considerable skill. And he knew the name of the crop. This made her curious. 'What d'you know about gardening?' she asked. 'Have you got a garden of your own?'

'Not any more. But I like gardening, and I know how rewarding it can be. And Pink Fir is a great salad potato.'

Perhaps she was tired. Suddenly it seemed quite normal for a specialist registrar she had only met a few hours before to be digging in her garden. But, still, she had to ask.

'Why did you come to see me? Is there something I should know?'

He paused, reached down and pulled a potato from one of the tines. 'Your house is on the way to where I was going. But I came because I wanted to see you and, yes, I do have an errand. However, basically I got out of the high dependency room only half an hour ago and I needed to calm down. I've been up nearly twenty hours, but I can't go to bed yet.'

'The high-dependency room?'

'We had a situation that turned into a problem that turned into an emergency that turned into a nightmare.'

'The woman you weren't sure about. You sent Freddy to check on her.'

'The very one. She was only thirty-odd weeks gone, the baby was very small and she had had kidney trouble before.'

'Don't tell me.' she said. 'Pre-eclampsia.'

'Quite right. An emergency section. There were times I thought we might lose her. But we didn't.'

'And the baby?'

He turned to smile at her. 'I guess you could say that the operation was a success. When I left mother and baby were doing well.'

It pleased her that he didn't mind showing that he was happy with the result. 'It gives you a good feeling when that happens,' she said. 'And you're very welcome to calm down here. But how did you know where I lived?'

'I listen to gossip,' he admitted cheerfully. 'Actually, Sister Reeves was telling me about you—about how well you did in training, who you shared with, how well she thought you'd coped this morning. Not that she'd ever tell *you* that.'

'Of course not,' Sue said.

'And I do have an errand. Young Freddy seems to think I might have some influence with you. He doesn't know that we were gossiping about him earlier. He wants me to persuade you come to Merry Stirling's do with him. Once again, let me say that I think him an upright and basically decent young man who in time will be a good doctor.'

She thought this was a mad conversation to be having after a twelve hour night shift. 'Would he come and dig up my Pink Fir potatoes?' she asked seriously.

Dan considered this question judiciously. 'If you asked him, he'd try,' he said. 'But, to be honest, I don't think he'd do as well as me. Incidentally, d'you want more fetching up?'

She had been enjoying their conversation and hadn't really noticed him digging. Now she realised just how much he had done—far more than she could have managed in the same time. He had worked economically, like an expert. He bent and lifted the little pink potatoes into the cardboard box she had put handy. There was a delicacy about the way he handled them, rubbing his fingers over the smooth skin as if the touch gave him pleasure. She shivered slightly as she involuntarily thought of his fingers touching her the same way.

'No, that's plenty,' she said hastily. 'Look, first of all, I don't want to go out with Freddy. I like him, but going out with him would only cause trouble because he'd want from me more than I can offer.'

He nodded, accepting that. 'It wasn't a job I wanted, because I didn't think there'd be much point,' he said. 'But I said I would ask, so I did.'

'That's settled. Now, I'm going to bed soon but first I'm going to have a mug of tea. D'you want one, too?'

'Love one. Anywhere I can wash my hands?'

She directed him to the downstairs washroom. She had put a tray ready for herself and the kettle had boiled. It only took a minute to reach for another mug. When he came out, smelling rather oddly of her scented soap, she was waiting, tray in hand. 'I thought, since it's getting to the end of summer, we might drink outside.'

'Great idea. We spend too much time indoors.'

'In hospital it's usually necessary,' she reminded him. Then suddenly she felt rather shy. 'I've built— grown—myself a little…arbour at the bottom of the garden. We can go there if you like. I…sit there a lot.'

'Somewhere special for you,' he said intuitively. 'I'd like to sit there, Sue.'

She led the way across the lawn to the bottom of the garden. Sometimes the other two girls came and sat out here with her, but mostly she sat here on her own. With a little shock she realised that this was the first man she had ever invited to come here with her. It had been her first project in the garden when she had bought the house four years ago. Here she could sit, secluded, and let all problems drift away.

'Fuchsias!' Dan exclaimed. 'You grow fuchsias! I love them, they're my favourite flower.'

They were walking along the Yorkshire stone path that led behind her greenhouse. Here, in a sunny but sheltered spot, she had a rockery and beds of her favourite flowers. They were still in bloom, red, white, pink, violet, variegated, a profusion of colour. He bent and touched a long salmon-coloured flower. 'This is Thalia, isn't it?'

Now she was amazed. 'Yes, it is. You know about vegetables and flowers. You must have been a gardener.'

'One of my dark secrets. I'll tell you more later.'

They turned a corner and then they were in her arbour. 'This is lovely,' he said quietly.

She had started by enclosing a small paved area in a square of tall fencing. Outside she had planted rapid-growing eucalyptus trees, and their silver trunks now hung over the fence top. Inside, shrub fuchsias grew, nearly hiding the brown of the wood behind. There was nothing to see but the trees, the flowers and the roof of the blue sky. Here she could be alone, here she was at peace.

She put the tray on the metal table and touched a switch hidden under the flowers. Water started to trickle down a cascade of stones in the corner, the gentle patter somehow emphasising the surrounding silence.

There was a wooden bench and two wooden chairs. She took a chair and Dan sat facing her. For a while they sat in silence, drinking their tea. She pushed the biscuit box over to him. 'Squashed flies,' he mumbled, and took a garibaldi.

There was a light dusting of hair on his forearms, a smear of earth on the otherwise pure white T-shirt. Sue could tell by the lines at the corners of his eyes that he had been up for hours, and he needed to sleep soon. His hair was an odd colour, and rather nice. She'd like to—

With a start she realised that she, too, was tired. She had been staring, perhaps rudely, at her guest, letting her thoughts wander pointlessly. When she realised he was smiling at her, noticing what she was doing, she didn't really mind.

'You escape here, don't you?' he asked. 'This is where you come when the world gets too much for you. For some women it's their bedroom or, indeed, their entire house, but for you it's this little corner. I'll bet you even sit out here in winter sometimes. All wrapped up in an overcoat.'

How did he know that? How did he guess? She nodded at the bird table in one corner. 'I bring bread and nuts for the birds,' she said. 'I love working in hospital but life there can get a bit…much sometimes. So I come here to relax.'

'Is it only life in hospital you're getting away from, Sue? Nothing else you're trying to ignore—or forget?'

This man was too shrewd! 'Only life in hospital,' she said briskly, though she suspected he didn't believe her. 'Some of the young mums we get, they have problems and you have to get involved a bit.'

'One of the difficult areas, deciding just how much you should get involved. You can't teach it—it has to be learned.'

She reached over for his now empty mug. 'Look, Dan, I…'

He held up his hand to forestall her. 'You've been up all night and you now need your sleep. So do I, and sitting here with you has made me an awful lot calmer. I'll go to my own bed.'

He stood, took the tray from her and they walked back up the garden. 'Are you going to invite me to your bower again?' he asked.

'Perhaps,' she said honestly. 'After all, we work together.'

'I can see why you want to keep it private.' He handed the tray to her outside the back door and she appreciated it that he wasn't going to try to come in again. 'Just one more thing. I know you finish your rotation tomorrow, then you've got a week off. Would you like to come out with me for the afternoon on

Sunday? Nothing exciting, just a little trip into the country and perhaps a small and dainty tea. But I'm certain you'll really enjoy yourself.'

'You're absolutely certain?' The derision was evident in her voice. She had known he was going to ask her something like this. For a moment she was tempted—he was an attractive man and she had enjoyed his company—but she was better off saying no to all men. She looked at him and there was a half smile on his face as if he knew what she was going to say.

He went on, 'Yes, I'm absolutely certain. Before you say no—or even yes—don't you want to know why I'm so certain?'

'I take it you're going to surprise me.'

'I am indeed. Young ladies in Victorian times used to take young men home to tea so their mothers could see if the gentleman in question was fiancé material. I propose to take you to see my father.'

'Your father! And to see if I'm fiancé material?' Now, this was unusual.

'Not at all to see if you are fiancé material. I propose to take you to see my father because you share a love of fuchsias.'

Something registered in the back of her mind. 'There's that expensive garden centre to the north of town. I've never been there but everyone's told me about it. A famous fuchsia-grower runs it—William Webster. He's not your father!'

'He certainly is,' Dan said cheerfully. 'So, if you won't come out with me for the pleasure of my company, will you come out with me to meet my father?'

'It's not that... I mean...' Suddenly she couldn't help herself. She yawned, massively. Fatigue hit her.

She was dog-tired, and if she didn't go to bed soon she'd just fall over. And no way could she make decisions.

'I'd love to meet you and your father,' she mumbled, 'but right now I—'

'Right now you're asleep on your feet. Not goodnight—good morning, Sue. I'll pick you up at two on Sunday. Oh, and last thing. Once again, you were good with that prolapse. See you.' And he was gone.

It took two minutes to rinse out the mugs and put everything away, then Sue stumbled upstairs to shower, brush her teeth and put on the expensive white silk pyjamas which were her sole luxury. Her bedroom windows were double-glazed, the curtains thick and well-fitting. She would sleep undisturbed. She found herself humming a song that had been popular over four years ago, 'He's my man, so keep your distance…' Then she stopped. What was she thinking of?

Why had she agreed to go out with Dan? She liked him, liked his energy, his enthusiasm. But he was a subtle man and could guess there were stories when other men would never have suspected. She'd have to be careful with him. And she was only going out with him so she could meet his father. Wasn't she?

Too much thinking. She closed her eyes and slept at once.

Fuchsias! As far as she could see, fuchsias. There were bushes, trailers, standards, pyramids. She thought she had a variety, but here there were types and colours she'd never dreamed of. The greenhouse stretched away in front of her and she just didn't know where to start looking.

'Dan said that you have a big garden of your own,'

William Webster said, 'and that you were particularly interested in fuchsias. I wouldn't have thought that a busy midwife had time.'

'I don't go out a lot,' she said, absorbed by a glorious mass of parti-coloured, bell-shaped blooms. 'I'd rather work on my flowers than go out gadding about.'

He looked at her approvingly. 'Me, too. My sons say I should get out more, meet more people. But why should I? I'm happy here in my greenhouse, or outside in the fields. Who needs people when you've got flowers?'

Sue thought that this was going a bit too far. 'But there are lots of people outside, buying stuff, drinking in that little café. You've got a thriving business here, you must meet people.'

'Hardly any at all,' William said cheerfully. 'A few people ask to meet me, fuchsia enthusiasts like yourself. I'm always happy to say hello to them. But I've got a partner, Phil Myers. He looks after the staff, money, sales—the business side. I look after the flowers. We get on well together.'

'You've got two sons, Dan and…Mickey, is it? Did neither of them want to go into business with you?'

William laughed and shook his head. 'No, although both of them have the makings of good gardeners. Still, I'm waiting for a fine crop of grandchildren. I'm sure one of them will want to take over the family firm. Now, come here and see what I'm working on at the moment.'

She was really enjoying herself, she realised as she followed William down the narrow aisle. Here there was that indefinable but exciting smell of dampness, growing plants and humus. And there were so many plants, so much beauty. William was an enthusiast, and though she was wary of enthusiasts she liked them. Although the older man was very different from his son, she could see certain character traits they had in common. A devotion to work for a start.

They passed through a double door at the end of the greenhouse after William had unlocked it carefully. This was a much smaller greenhouse, with a powerful artificial heating system overhead. William pointed to a series of small plants in a tray of sand. 'This is where I try to breed new species. I've had three or four successes. You know Sweet Elizabeth?'

'Yes. It's a small, delicate plant, with a beautiful pink and white flower.'

'I bred that. I named it after my wife—she liked flowers. And now I'm trying to produce one that's so white as to be almost silver.'

'Silver,' she said, and he didn't notice the strain in her voice.

He went on to explain the complex process of trying to breed a new strain, and she became more and more fascinated. 'Anyone can do it,' he said. 'It only takes time and care.'

'I'd love to create a complete new plant. But I promised myself that I'd do nothing extra this first year. I'm still learning, William. But after this year I'd like to try. Could I come back and talk to you then?'

'You'll always be welcome here. I like talking to people who share my interests.'

After they'd walked back into the main greenhouse he picked up one of the trolleys that were available for customers and started to drop plants into it. 'What are you doing?' Sue asked, though she had a good idea.

'Just a few plants for your garden,' he said. 'I'm picking the ones that should fit your situation.'

'William, I can't accept all these! I mean, this is your livelihood—you grow these to sell.'

'When you get to my age you find it's fun to give things away. Especially to people who appreciate them. I want you to have these and—'

'Grandad, Grandad!'

The door at the far end of the greenhouse opened and towards them hurtled two tiny figures, a boy and a girl. William stooped to pick them up, one in each arm. 'These are my first grandchildren,' he told Sue proudly. 'This is Stephen and this is Helen. They're twins. Aren't they lovely?'

'They are, indeed. Can I have a kiss, Stephen and Helen?' Helen was willing enough, but Stephen was shy and turned away his head.

'A midwife's work finishes a month after the birth,' Sue said, 'so you help bring a baby into the world and then it's lost to you. Sometimes I think it's a pity. I'd like to know how they get on. I'd like to see more of children like Helen and...'

Something was nagging at her. Suddenly it came back. 'Helen and Stephen Webster! Mother, Alice Webster. William, I've met this little pair before! I was training, helping the midwife who delivered them. I remember now. Alice gave me a big box of chocolates and sent me a very nice note.'

'I knew you were going to be a good midwife,' another voice said, 'Sue, it's good to see you again.'

Sue turned to meet Alice Webster, an attractive blonde lady in dark trousers and a floral blouse. Smiling at her side was Dan. While William had shown Sue round the greenhouse he'd stayed behind to wait for his sister-in-law.

'So you were the student midwife when Alice produced these two rascals?' he asked.

'I was. But I don't remember you being around.'

'I was in America for three months. When I came back I was an uncle.'

'Uncle Dan!' shouted Stephen, and leaned forward to dive into Dan's waiting arms.

The little group turned to walk back to the house. 'So, how is the midwife who looked after me?' Alice asked. 'Gemma Penrose. She was good, too. In fact, you were a good team.'

'Gemma is fine. I see a lot of her. Actually, she's coming round to tea next Saturday. I'm glad Helen and Stephen have turned out so well. You know, I never knew that that attractive man who came to see you was Dan's brother. The name's the same but it just never registered.'

'Mickey's just like Dan,' smiled Alice. 'A different trade, but he's just as dedicated to it. Mickey's a police inspector.'

'What sort of policeman is he?'

'He's in charge of the drugs squad, believe it or not.'

Sue couldn't help it—she twitched when she heard that. And she felt sure that Dan had noticed.

William had prepared a tea that was delicious—he told Sue that they kept a section of the garden centre for producing vegetables and salad that were solely for the staff's use. And they also reared a few free-range hens. Sue thought she'd never had such an enjoyable meal. After a while Helen came to sit on her knee, and Sue made her a tiny egg sandwich.

She felt at home here. There was a warmth in the

atmosphere. William, Alice and Dan were obviously all very fond of each other, and Sue found herself wishing that Mickey had been here, too. But he was an inspector in charge of the drugs squad. He'd have to be hard. Perhaps he wasn't. Sue couldn't see Alice being happy with a man who was hard.

After tea Alice and Dan sat to talk about the children and Sue insisted on helping William in the kitchen. The more she saw of William the more he reminded her of Dan. His hair was grey, but his body was still lean. He wasn't as outgoing as Dan, but she felt that underneath he was just as kind.

She washed the dishes, he wiped and put away. For a while they worked together in companionable silence.

'Has Dan told you anything about his mother?' William asked after a while.

Sue looked at him cautiously, thinking this might be a delicate subject. 'No, he hasn't. In fact, we haven't…known each other for very long.'

'That's interesting. He usually only brings old friends to come to see me. Anyway…' He reached into a drawer and brought out a picture. 'There's a picture of Elizabeth in every room in this house, but I don't have them out. She's been dead fifteen years and I still miss her.'

Sue studied the picture. There was a suggestion of Dan about Elizabeth Webster's eyes and in the line of her forehead. 'She was very beautiful,' she said. 'What did she…? I mean…'

William guessed what she was asking. 'She was forty-five and she was pregnant,' he said, a sad smile on his face. 'I was going to be a father again at fifty, and we were all delighted. Dan was away in the depths of Africa doing his elective in a tiny bush village when his mother had…complications. She died even before he could be told. She was buried before he came home.'

'You're telling me this for a reason, aren't you?' she asked.

'Possibly. I think Dan went into the speciality he did because of his mother. Before that he wanted to be a surgeon. And I think the way he rushes round, trying to do everyone's job, is because he never really said goodbye to her. He thinks it's almost his fault.'

'He might have at first. But surely by now he will have realised that's not true.' Sue was intrigued by this idea.

'Again, possibly. But he's never started any long term relationship with a girl, never got the same happiness that Mickey gets out of his marriage. Perhaps he's afraid of falling in love and then losing everything. I just don't know.'

Sue was even more intrigued. The last thing she had thought Dan might be was vulnerable. He seemed to be tough, on top of every situation. But then, she didn't know him very well. Not yet.

'Let's go back and sit with the others,' William said. 'I know Alice will have to be off soon.'

It was while Sue was helping Alice button the children into their coats that the idea came. It was something she had never done before—but she had so enjoyed being with this family that she wanted somehow to show her thanks.

'Next Saturday,' she said, 'as you know I'm having a friend Gemma round to tea. Would you all like to come as well? If it's fine the children could play in my garden. And, Alice, could you bring Mickey?'

Like any family, they all looked at each other, before answering. Then there was a cautious affirmative murmuring. 'Can't ever vouch for Mickey,' Alice said, 'but I'd love to come with the children.' So it was arranged. Sue found herself half-frightened at what she had done. It just wasn't like her.

'You enjoyed yourself,' Dan said as he drove her home, 'and so did I.'

'I enjoyed myself more than you can imagine,' Sue said, 'I really envy you your family.' Then she realised that that had been careless, and it made his next question almost inevitable.

'You have no family yourself?'

'No.'

There was silence for a moment, then he said, 'I can tell by the curt answer that there's some story there. But you don't want to tell me. That's fine, but I'd like to hear, and someday you might want to confide.'

'It's possible. But it won't be yet.'

They were in the city now, and although Dan chatted away happily she was aware that her answers were getting shorter and more ungracious. She couldn't help it. She was apprehensive.

Eventually Dan said, 'We're nearly at your home now. I'm glad you got on so well with my family— they liked you a lot. And I want to see more of you.'

He turned to glance at her, seeing her serious face. 'But, Sue, we've got all the time in the world. I'm not a really young man like Freddy, and I can see that you've got...difficulties. I want to help you with them.'

'What difficulties do I have?' she flared, 'And, if I do, who says I need help with them?'

He was still calm. 'I don't know what difficulties you might have. And at some time everyone needs help.'

'Why pick on me? There must be dozens of girls you could take out if you wanted.'

'Possibly so. But none of them would get on with my family as well as you have. Besides, I think I like you.'

He pulled up outside her house. 'Normally,' he said, 'you would invite me in for coffee, I would kiss you goodnight and we'd arrange another date. But you're all tense, you're nervous—I can feel it. So I'll say straight away that I'm not coming in. I've enjoyed this afternoon, and I'm looking forward to seeing you next week.'

She sat, silent, irresolute. 'Please, come in for a quick coffee,' she said. 'And I'm not just being polite—I would like you to come in.'

He didn't move. 'I'd like that. Will you tell me about yourself—in time?'

'I don't think so. Not all of it. The past is better dead and forgotten. Now, d'you want this coffee?'

'I certainly do,' he said courteously.

CHAPTER THREE

SUE knew that one of the disadvantages of living so close to the hospital, and being known to have no family, was that if there was an emergency she would be one of the first to be called out. It didn't happen very often. But apparently two midwives were off ill and one was on holiday. Unusually, there were none available from the bank, the register of available medical staff.

'If you could come in for a late this afternoon,' a desperate shift leader phoned to say, 'we'd be very grateful. You can either have another shift off in lieu, or you can be paid overtime. But, please, can you get here?'

'I'll be there,' Sue said laconically. 'Pencil me in.' A late—an afternoon—lasted from a quarter past two until a quarter to ten. For various reasons it was often the busiest of shifts.

She arrived in plenty of time for handover and was given Tracy Sheean by the departing midwife. 'Nothing much happening yet,' the midwife said as she passed on the notes, 'and you're welcome to her.'

'Like that, is it?' Sue said glumly. Some mums-to-be were wonderful, the vast majority were all right, but some were a pain. Still, she didn't expect to be able to choose her patients.

Tracy was aged nineteen, had lank hair, poor teeth and a neglected body. Sue saw from the earlier midwife's report that she had missed nearly all of the antenatal visits. And now, not really knowing what to expect, she was terrified. She was terrified of the pain and terrified, too, of the Entonox machine. 'I don't like gas, don't give me gas,' she whined. 'But it hurts ever so much. Can't you give me an injection or something?'

'I'm afraid not. We don't have anything like that.' When conducting her preliminary examination, Sue had looked at the girl's arms to see if there were the track marks that indicated drug abuse. Fortunately there were none—though that didn't mean that Tracy hadn't been a user. So she tried to get the girl to relax, tried to explain what was happening so that Tracy could deal with what was coming. But Tracy was beyond reason. 'Me Nan said that it had to hurt,' she said. 'Having babies always hurts.'

'It would hurt less if you could do as I tell you,' Sue said patiently. 'Try not to tense up. I know it's hard but it'll make things easier for you. And try to breathe as I told you.' When I'm Prime Minister, she thought to herself, I'll make non-attendance at antenatal classes a criminal offence.

The one good thing was that the labour seemed to be progressing perfectly. Vital signs were fine—this should be a textbook delivery.

'Is anyone coming in to see you?' Sue asked casually after a while. 'Anyone I could phone perhaps?' Somehow, by soothing talk and refusing to lose her temper, she had managed to calm Tracy down a little. What was needed now was someone else to hold Tracy's hand, to mop her forehead and talk to her, make her feel loved. A partner or a mother. The suggestion hadn't been a good one. Tracy had found something else to worry about.

'I want Frankie,' she gasped. 'I want Frankie. Where's me feller? They said when the ambulance came that they'd tell him I was coming here.'

'Is Frankie at work?' Sue asked delicately. 'Can I phone there to tell him?'

But it turned out that Frankie didn't exactly work and, although he was out doing something, there was no way of contacting him.

The afternoon wore on, with Tracy being one of the worst patients Sue had ever had. She could not be left alone. When there was a comparatively quiet period, and Sue tried to slip out for a coffee, there was an instant screamed objection. 'You can't leave me now! You've got to be here to look after me!' Then there was a tearful apology. 'I'm sorry, Sue. You're good to me, but don't leave me.' Sue sighed.

When the labour was well on its way, long after he would have been able to offer comfort and support, Frankie arrived. He was a small man in a greasy black leather jacket, with slicked-back hair.

Sue took the opportunity to slip out when he came in, and had what she thought was a well-earned rest and a coffee. When she got back to the delivery room Frankie turned on her. 'Where's the doctor in charge here? I want a word. This girl needs more painkillers.'

'We have Entonox for her—gas and air. She already knows how to take it herself.'

'She needs more than that. Can't you tell she's suffering? Get me the doctor.'

Sue repressed the urge to point out that if Tracy had attended a few antenatal classes, she would be suffering less. Instead, she said, 'I'm afraid all births involve a certain amount of discomfort. We can't wipe out all pain. But if you want a word, there will be a doctor along in a few minutes.' She knew that Freddy would drop in shortly. He could try to deal with this man, and good luck to him.

She leaned over and checked the monitor and Tracy's condition. Everything seemed to be going well. She filled in the relevant section of the partogram. Then, as she stepped back, Frankie shouted, 'I said I want a doctor here and I want him quickly.'

'You're disturbing my patient. Keep your voice down.' Sue turned and left the room. If Freddy was around he could come in now.

Frankie followed her quickly. 'Don't you walk away from me. I haven't finished talking to you yet. Now, I said I wanted a doctor. So get me one!' Then he did the unforgivable. He poked her on the shoulder.

Sue swung back towards him so the man had to give way, even move backwards until he was against the corridor wall. She put her face close to his and snarled, 'I'll get the doctor when *I* think it's necessary. Don't interfere when you don't know what you're talking about. And the next time you touch me I'll ring for Security and have you thrown out. I know you're on something and the chances are you're stupid enough to be still carrying it.'

She saw fear flash in his eyes and knew that her guess had been a lucky one. 'Now get out of here and throw it down the nearest drain. Then come back and behave yourself.' She stepped aside to let him move.

He tried to retrieve some of his pride. 'You can't talk to me like that. I'll make a—'

She held up her bleeper. 'Out, or I call Security. They won't be as nice to you as I am.'

For a moment they glared at each other. Then

Frankie's gaze dropped, and he turned and walked away.

She watched him until the corridor door shut behind him, and heaved a sigh of relief. Then she jumped as a voice behind her said, 'That was remarkable, Sue.'

She turned, to see Dan, dressed casually in jeans. He wasn't smiling as he usually did, and there was a thoughtful expression on his face. 'You startled me,' she said accusingly. 'Where did you come from?'

He indicated the office door behind him. 'Just came down to check some records. I wasn't eavesdropping but I heard everything you said to that man. Sue, you took too big a risk. We've got Security for people like that—it's not a midwife's job. Are you OK?'

'I'm fine. I'm just angry. And when I can't sort out a man like that, I'll give up.'

His thoughtful expression hadn't changed. 'Not every father-to-be that we get in here is entirely adequate,' he said. 'We all know and accept that. But it was the drugs that upset you wasn't it?'

'Yes! If I had my way I'd hang all drug dealers. What chance have that mother and child got when there's someone selling drugs on the doorstep every day?'

She took a deep breath. It wasn't often these days that she got so angry, so out of control. Perhaps dealing with the awkward Tracy had tired her more than she'd realised. 'Sorry,' she said. 'Sometimes I get carried away.'

'Everyone here dislikes drugs and what they can do. But you dislike them more than most. Any special reason?'

'Just my little hobby-horse. Not important.'

'I see. Well, since you're out in the corridor, what

about a coffee? And what are you doing in here now?
I thought you were on lates.'

This was safer ground. 'No time for coffee. I've got
one of the awkward brigade as a mum-to-be. And I
got called in to do an extra shift as an emergency.'
She thought for a moment and added, 'If that girl in
there had a family anything like yours, she wouldn't
be in this mess now.'

'That's nice to hear. I'm glad you liked them, Sue.'

Rapidly she walked back into the delivery room.
She felt that she'd given away more than she'd intended to Dan. He was a shrewd man, she didn't want
him finding out more.

Incredibly, things got better. After about an hour
there was a knock on the door, and there was Frankie,
pale-faced and abject. He was carrying a sheaf of
sweet peas, obviously bought from the kiosk in the
hospital foyer, and a paper carrier.

'I'd like to come in now, Nurse, if it's all right,' he
mumbled. 'Sorry about before. I wasn't quite myself,
you know. Worried and that.'

'You're very welcome,' Sue said. 'Why don't you
go and hold Tracy's hand? She's been wanting you.'

Frankie dropped the carrier against the wall, thrust
the flowers at her and said, 'Bought these.' Then he
moved rapidly and seized Tracy's hand. Tracy was
overjoyed. Sue found a vase and put the flowers in the
far corner of the room.

After that the birth was surprisingly straightforward.
Just at the right time Sue rang for another midwife to
join her, and shortly afterwards Tracy produced a large
baby boy. 'Look! I want to call him Frankie,' she
gasped.

'He's a lovely baby,' Sue said, 'and that's a lovely

name.' She could see the delight in Tracy's eyes—
and, surprisingly, also Frankie's eyes.

There was the necessary paperwork to finish, and
then a trolley to take mother and child along to the
maternity ward. A job well done. Just as he left the
delivery room, Frankie grabbed the paper carrier and
took something from it. He handed Sue a box of chocolates.

'Sorry again,' he said. 'Me, the baby and Tracy
want you to have these.'

Sue took the box. 'Well, thank you,' she said.
Although it was taking a risk, and not really her business, she went on, 'Now, look, Frankie, this is Tracy's
first baby, and she's going to need a lot of support.
You've got to make sure she does what the midwife
and the health visitor say. She—they—will be relying
on you.'

'Yes…yes, I know. I'll do what I can.' And he was
gone.

Sue looked after him in surprise for a moment, then
shrugged. There was the partogram to finish.

Eventually, there was time for coffee. Unusually, there
was no one to gossip to. The room was empty. Sue
poured herself a cup and wandered round, flipping
over magazines. She must be happy, she thought to
herself, she was singing. The words came back to her.
'He's my man, so keep your distance, he's my man,
he don't need you. I love my man…'

A voice said, 'I seem to be spending my time creeping up on you. Sue, you have a gorgeous voice.'

It was Dan again, this time dressed in greens. She
flushed. She didn't like people to hear her singing.
'What are you doing still here?' she snapped.

He ignored her bad-tempered tone. 'I've been in Theatre, assisting in a forceps delivery that turned into a section. I didn't have to stay, it wasn't my operation, but the junior reg who was doing it said that if I had nothing better to do I could hang around. I judged those casual words to be a desperate cry for help. So I did stay. And there was absolutely no need—he did fine.'

'I see. Can I pour you a coffee?'

'Love one.' He took the cup, slumped into a chair and looked at her with alert eyes. 'You know I'm help-ing to organise a concert to raise money for the hos-pital fund?'

'Yes. I've heard. So you're an impresario as well as a registrar and a gardener.'

'I like to think I can turn my hand to anything,' he said modestly. 'Now, you know we've got a choir?'

She was uneasy, she knew what was coming. 'Yes, my friend Jane is in it. But you know I'm very busy and—'

'Everyone's very busy.' He swept aside what she was going to say. 'We're short of alto voices. I've just heard you sing and if you could come and audition you—'

'No!' Her answer came at once, too quickly.

'There won't be too much work,' he said placat-ingly, 'and I'm sure you—'

'No. Don't ask me, it's just not my thing. I can't sing. I'll happily help behind the scenes, though. You must want someone to do that.'

For a moment she thought she saw annoyance on his face. But it swiftly disappeared and he looked thoughtful again. 'We do want someone to act as as-sistant stage manager, thought not as much as we need voices for the choir. But thanks for your offer anyway. I'll take you up on it.'

She knew she had let something slip. This man was far too shrewd, she thought again! 'I'd better go,' she said.

She was looking forward to her party on Saturday. Jane and Megan would be away and she would have the house to herself. She planned her menu, then spent extra hours trying to make the garden look good. If she was to show William round, she wanted everything to be perfect!

Then on Thursday morning there was a sad telephone call from Alice. 'I hung on a couple of days, hoping I was wrong, but I'm not. The kids have got chickenpox. There's no way I can bring them round to your place, and they're so miserable I daren't leave them so I don't think I can come myself. Sue, we were all looking forward to it!'

'Alice, I'm so sorry. I know what kids with chickenpox can be like. Anything I can do?'

'Thanks anyway, but no. Looking after kids when they're ill is part of the contract, isn't it? One of the things mothers have to accept. And Mickey's very good.' Alice paused a minute and then said, too casually, 'Seen anything of Dan recently?'

'I'm always running into him. We work the same set of rooms.'

'Well, he'll be popping round soon to see us. Get him to bring you if you've time. The kids love their uncle.'

'I can imagine it. There's something uncle-like about him.'

'He's a lovely man—take a sister-in-law's word for it. If I didn't have Mickey...'

Over the phone Sue heard the sound of distant screams. Alice sighed. 'Mother's needed again. Hope to see you soon Sue.' She rang off.

Sue paused, then rang Dan. 'Do you still want to come?' she asked, after explaining that Alice and the children wouldn't be able to.

'Very much so,' he said, 'and I know Dad is looking forward to it. Are you sure you don't want to cancel?'

'No,' she said, 'I don't want to cancel.'

'Good. Incidentally, I meant to ask. Shall I bring some wine?'

'That would be nice. I tend to forget it. I hardly drink at all myself.'

'It'll be nice, having dinner with you, Sue.' And he rang off.

Her first idea had been to have a buffet so that the children could enjoy themselves and both eat and run about. But since she was now down to herself and three guests—Gemma, William and Dan—she decided to have a more formal meal. When she had time, when she had someone to cater for, she liked cooking.

Her garden was now as perfect as it would ever be. On Saturday morning she started on the house and the meal. She put a pretty flower arrangement in the centre of the dining-room table and another on the sideboard. Her own flowers, of course. She decided on a salad for the first course, baked trout, new potatoes, peas and broccoli as a main course, then fresh fruit salad and cheese to follow. With only one hot course she could spent more time with her guests. Dan had said he would bring wine, but she was the hostess so she should provide some. She went to the supermarket and bought a bottle of white which the assistant assured her would go well with fish.

The garden, the room, the meal— all were ready. And she had plenty of time. She went upstairs, bathed and tried to decide what to wear. There was a blue silk dress hanging in her wardrobe, bought on impulse years ago and never yet worn. She didn't wear fancy clothes much these days. After all, she seldom went out.

She wriggled into the dress and surveyed herself in the mirror. She had to admit she looked good in it. The blue went well with her colouring. For a treat she put on make-up, a little more than usual. Just for to-night, she thought, because I'm looking forward to it. It was so long since she had been a party animal. Now she was remembering that dressing up could be fun.

Gemma arrived first. She was early, and called into the open hall, 'It's me. Shall I come in?'

'I'm in the kitchen,' Sue shouted back, prodding the broccoli with a fork.

'It's a lovely afternoon so I walked through the park,' Gemma said, plonking a bottle of red wine on the table. 'My, don't you look wonderful? Is Mr Right coming?'

'No,' said Sue, feeling slightly warm. 'Just a friend and his father. I'm afraid the others couldn't come. Anyway, you look very good yourself.'

Her friend was wearing a calf-length cocktail dress in black. She was subtly but well made-up, her hair freshly done. Sue knew she was into her fifties, but her figure and face could have passed for someone ten years younger.

'Have to make an effort sometimes,' Gemma said cheerfully. 'I've been out on the district all week, and I'm fed up with wearing the uniform and shouting at rather dim mothers.'

She was a competent, experienced midwife, and Sue counted herself lucky that Gemma had been her mentor in the hospital. The two were now firm friends.

'I think this will do,' Sue said. 'Come on, we'll sit in the front room and gossip.'

The next to arrive was William, driving a dusty Land Rover. As she met him on the doorstep he handed her a bunch of flowers. 'These are from my garden,' he said. Then he stooped and picked up a cardboard box. 'And so are these, but I don't know quite how to present them.'

Sue looked in the box and blinked. It was full of vegetables, still with the soil clinging to them. They smelled glorious. 'William, thank you,' she said. 'I mean, no one has—'

'No one has ever brought you vegetables as a present?' he asked. 'Perhaps I can start a trend.'

'It'll be a good one,' she said. 'Come on in and meet Gemma.'

William looked different. It was a bit of a shock. When she'd met him before he'd had on jeans and a dark shirt, suitable for working in the greenhouse. Now he was wearing a light grey suit, with a white shirt and a floral tie. He looked a different man. With a shock she realised he was handsome. Some errant part of her mind wondered if this was how Dan would look in twenty-five years. If so, he would be lucky.

'My friend, Gemma Penrose, who delivered your two grandchildren,' she said as they entered the living room. 'And this is William Webster, who owns the big nursery to the north of town.'

Neither of her two guests paid any attention to her. Gemma rose, held out her hand and William took it in both of his. 'How nice to meet you,' William said. 'I've been so much looking forward to it.'

'I think I have, too,' Gemma replied, showing no signs of wanting to take her hand back. 'So you're the Webster of Webster's Nurseries. I live in a flat so I have no garden, but I'd love to grow flowers.'

'There are always indoor plants,' William said, as she drew him to sit beside her on the couch. 'Let's have a think about it.'

Sue thought she could almost see the spark that flashed between them. She knew that Gemma had been married once—had been divorced and glad of it, she'd told Sue bitterly. But now it was obvious that she could be attracted to the right man. And could attract him in her turn.

'I'll just see to things in the kitchen,' Sue mumbled. 'You two talk.' It was obvious they intended to do just that.

The bell rang, and she went to let in Dan. Her heart bumped when she saw him—that was ridiculous. She barely knew him. But it did. He, too, was dressed semi-formally, in a lightweight blue suit, with a fashionable dark shirt and a floral tie like his father's.

'You look stunning,' he said. 'Why don't you dress like that more often?'

'Because I wear a uniform most days,' she said pertly, 'and the rest of the time I like to relax.'

'I see.' He presented her with a bag. 'Inside there's a bottle of wine, wrapped in wet paper to try to keep it cool. I didn't bring you flowers, I knew my father would and I just can't compete.' Then he gave her another parcel wrapped in shiny red paper, about two feet long. 'So here is another present.'

Whatever could it be? What could he give her that

was two feet long? 'For me? I'm going to open it now.'

He shook his head. 'Keep it till later. There'll be a better time then.'

That intrigued her, but she would do as he'd suggested. 'Come into the front room,' she said, 'and I'll serve everyone a drink.'

They all had a glass of the white wine she had bought and chatted for a while. Dan, of course, had met Gemma often before and obviously thought her a fine midwife. After a while William asked if they could all look round her garden and Gemma said that she'd like to look, too.

By the time they had finished their little tour Sue felt a rosy glow of pleasure. William was very complimentary about what he saw, and she was sure he was being sincere. He also gave her a couple of ideas. She was so glad she had invited him!

It was a good meal. Everyone said so, and Sue felt that she had to agree with them. Dan suggested that they try the wine he had brought, and she found herself thoroughly enjoying it. They ate, they drank, they chatted. A happy, civilised meal.

Just as she was serving coffee the doorbell rang again. Rather surprised, Sue opened the door, and there on the step was a darker, tougher-looking version of Dan. She remembered him at once. It was Mickey, Alice's husband!

'Sorry we couldn't come to the party,' he said, 'but I've just dropped in to say hello.' He smiled, and hefted a green box. 'And I've brought some after-dinner mints.' His tough, wary expression disappeared when he smiled, and it became obvious he was Dan's brother.

'You're just in time for a glass of wine and a cup of coffee,' Sue said. She accepted the green box. 'And perhaps an after-dinner mint as well.'

Mickey stayed for an hour, and told them that the children were improving slightly. Then he went to relieve Alice. Shortly afterwards Gemma said that she, too, ought to be going as she had a busy day tomorrow. 'I'll run you home,' said Dan, when he realised that she had walked there.

'No, time I was going, too,' William said firmly. 'I'll run you home.'

'That would be very nice of you, William,' said Gemma demurely.

'You arranged that,' Dan accused Sue with a grin when the two had left. 'You brought them together on purpose.'

'Not entirely. I had already invited Gemma to tea. But it did strike me that they might quite...like each other. Why, d'you mind?'

'Not at all, I'm delighted. Sometimes we tend to think that those older than us are incapable of the same feelings, urges, that we have. And it's wrong, isn't it?'

'Yes,' she said, blushing, 'it's wrong.'

'We shouldn't say of anyone that they're past feeling desire. Especially, we shouldn't say it of ourselves.'

'I think you're getting off the point,' she said. 'We were talking of your father and Gemma.'

'We were? Of course we were.' He looked out of the window. 'See, dusk's coming on, but I don't think it's a cold night.' He lifted his glass. 'We could take our drinks into your arbour.'

'All right. I'd like that. I'll fetch a blanket to put on the bench.'

'And before we go out you should unwrap your present.'

She had forgotten it. She went into the hall and returned with the long red parcel.

'I love surprises,' she said. 'Well, I love nice surprises.'

The paper was soon torn off. There, in cardboard containers, were two giant candles. 'They're meant to be lit outdoors,' he said. 'I thought you might like candlelight in your arbour.'

'Dan, what a lovely idea! I want to take them out right now! Come on, bring the bottle and glasses and I'll bring the candles and blanket.'

She spread the blanket on the bench as he carefully bedded in the candles and then lit them. She sat at one end of the bench, and Dan poured them both a glass of wine. 'Just this one,' she told him, 'and then no more.'

'You're very careful not to drink too much,' he told her, 'even though you're at home. Is there a special reason for it?'

'Yes. There's a special reason.'

He came and sat on the bench, not by her but at the opposite end. It had got darker quite quickly, and the light of the candles flickered, making his face a thing of planes and shadows. She watched him gravely, liking the effect. There was a moment's contented silence as he sipped his wine.

'I've got a confession to make,' he said, not looking at her. 'I hope you'll still like me afterwards.'

'Tell me your guilty secret.' She hoped it wasn't something too bad.

'You must know I'm curious about you,' he said. 'I'm intrigued by the contrast between you as a...very attractive young woman and someone who doesn't apparently want anything to do with men.'

She didn't like that. 'Why do all men think that if you don't want to go out with them there must be something wrong with you?'

He didn't answer her question. Instead, he said, 'I managed to see your application form for your hospital job.'

'Did you?' she said coldly. 'I thought they were supposed to be confidential.'

'I'm entitled to look as I'm on the academic board. But what I found was that there was a gap of three years between you leaving school and starting here. You had the exam results to start as a midwife, but you didn't. I think those three years are significant.'

'I hate the idea of being spied on!'

He lifted his hands in apology. 'And I hate spying. But I did it for you. There's something and it's getting between you and me and I don't want it to. So, will you tell me, Sue?'

She realised that he was a man who wouldn't give up, and a little part of her was pleased that someone should care so much for her that he would go to all this trouble. But could she tell him? It was something she had hidden away for so long. She glanced round the arbour she had built to hide herself in. It was comforting as always, the more so because of the candlelight. But now there was someone else in her arbour, someone she had invited. She made up her mind.

'I've told no one else this,' she said. 'No one in this hospital, no one in this entire city knows anything about it. Not Gemma or anyone. If I tell you, you're not to question me or ask me to talk about it. I couldn't stand that.'

'Talking sometimes helps. But you know you can trust me. I hope you do,' he said quietly.

'Trust! You picked the wrong word there.' After that quick exclamation her voice dropped to a low monotone. 'I trusted someone before.'

After a pause she went on, 'I envied you, Dan—in fact, I still envy you because you've got a family. I haven't. My own mother died when I was very young. My father brought me up as best he could—at least, I presume he thought so. He was a cold man. I spent most of my childhood being shunted between baby-minders and nannies and housekeepers—anyone he could hire to keep me out of his way. I wasn't abused or harmed in any way, you understand. I just wasn't loved.

'Then, when I was fifteen, my father remarried, and I hoped I'd have a family at last. But the woman my father married didn't care much for me, though she pretended. She had a son of her own called Nigel. She much preferred him to me, and he was better than me at manipulating her. Any trouble, and I got the blame.'

Dan didn't say anything, or move towards her. Some part of her appreciated that. He knew that the last thing she needed now was human contact.

'Anyway, my dad died. The three of us struggled along somehow together—my stepmother needed me to get at the money my father had left. Then when I was eighteen she just upped and emigrated to Australia. Never heard of again. I got a job in the music industry. I suppose I was young and good-looking, and I accepted the first offer of marriage that came my way. I married Doug Jones.' The words were spat out.

'I didn't know at the time, but he was into drugs.

Not just using, but dealing as well, I think. A little bit anyway.' She stopped. This was the hardest part of her story, but it was where she daren't tell all.

'Anyway, he was a…louse. I worked and he spent the money. Then he died, too. A car crash—he was drunk at the time. And I'm glad he's dead!'

She knew her voice was rising now, the tears running down her face. So much of this she had thrust down, tried to forget. Talking about it again hurt more than razor cuts. Would the pain never go away?

'So he was dead—and I was two months pregnant. For a while, just a little while, I was happy. I was going to have a baby of my own. I did everything right. I had the right diet, plenty of sleep, consulted my doctor. Then I had pains, and I knew they weren't normal. I went to the doctor.

'There was still a reasonable chance that everything might be all right. But it wasn't. At five months the baby was born—dead. For five months I had carried him. I asked—it was a boy. So now I help woman have babies, and I don't judge any of them in case they might have a story like mine. And I distrust all men.'

The last words were wailed. She turned to him. He made as if to move towards her and then checked himself. She was glad of that. Instead, he took out his handkerchief and held it out for her. It took a while, but eventually the tears and the sobs subsided. 'I'm all right now,' she said. 'Well, sort of.'

'There's nothing I can say,' he told her sadly. 'Except, of course, that I'm so so sorry for you. I know it doesn't help much, but I think even your story could have a happy ending.' He frowned, and his voice was thoughtful. 'I think there's more to the story than you've told me, but that's fine—you can tell me the rest when you're ready. You know I'll do whatever I can for you.'

For a while there was silence. Then she said, 'You can hold my hand if you like.'

He moved along the bench and took her hand in his. It was warm, comforting. After a while he put his arm round her shoulders. To her surprise she didn't mind. There was something reassuring about Dan. Finally he kissed her, not the demanding kiss of a lover but the loving kiss of someone who cared for her. She lay against him, and felt almost happy.

CHAPTER FOUR

THE first shift back on nights was always tiring. It took time for Sue's body to adjust, to move from living and working during the day to staying up all night. The day-shift midwives she met at handover seemed to be more cheerful than they had any right to be.

'Mum's called Pat Knowles—she's well into the first stage,' the departing midwife said. 'She's due for an internal, but I thought I'd leave it to you.'

'No problem,' Sue said. If a midwife was coming to the end of her shift, she would often leave an internal examination to the relieving midwife. It saved the mother-to-be the discomfort of two examinations.

'I think you're well into the second stage now,' Sue said some ten minutes later. 'You're fully dilated, so you're on the last stretch now.'

'I'm glad about that,' Pat panted.

But after three hours there didn't seem to be too much progress. Pat was tiring rapidly. She wasn't a strong woman and she was nearing exhaustion. And if not exactly worried, Sue was concerned about the baby. She had attached an FSE—a foetal scalp electrode— to the baby's head as the readings from it were far more accurate than those from the sensors placed on the mother's abdomen. The baby's head was being compressed now, and it was to be expected that there would be some deceleration in heartbeat. But the decelerations were late—after the contraction—and didn't return to the baseline as quickly as Sue would have liked.

'I think we'll have the doctor in.' She smiled at Pat. 'Let him see how you're getting on.' She buzzed for Freddy.

Freddy could always be relied on to be professional, and he was a kind and courteous man, too. He said hello to Pat, before looking at the partogram, and then took Sue aside to hear what she had to say. Then he examined the patient, smiling reassuringly as he did so.

'I don't think there's anything seriously wrong,' he said to Sue afterwards, 'but this child is in no great hurry to be born and I think we should give him or her a helping hand. Or, to be exact, a helping suck.'

'A ventouse extraction.' Sue nodded, and went to get the equipment.

Sue sat by her patient and explained what was going to happen. 'Baby isn't coming quite quickly enough so the doctor will put a cup on the head, and create a vacuum inside it. Then when you have a contraction and push, he'll be able to ease the baby downwards.'

'It won't hurt the baby?'

'Certainly not, Pat. It's a very simple procedure.'

Sue was pleased to see that Freddy was taking his time, ensuring that the cup was in the right position and waiting until the vaccum was at the right level. In a previous birth she had seen a cup come off. There had been no danger to mother or child but it had been a disturbing thing to happen.

'Ready now,' he called. 'At the next contraction, Pat.'

Once again Freddy got things right. There was no

attempt to pull the baby out, but a gentle easing. The head rotated just as in a normal birth.

'And here we go! Pat, you've got a daughter!'

There was more reassurance necessary. Because the baby's scalp was still slightly mobile, the vacuum had caused some of it to rise in what was called a chignon. 'Don't worry, it's only bruising,' Sue explained. 'It'll all go down in the next few days.'

She liked working with Freddy. He was a good doctor.

At the end of the shift Sue felt exhausted. But then she saw Dan walking towards her down the corridor and suddenly the world seemed a brighter place. He was dressed casually in jeans and a T-shirt, not his normal clinical wear. It was only thirty-six hours since they had sat together in her arbour, but she had thought about him rather a lot. She knew she would have to think more.

There were other midwives ahead of her, and as usual Dan had a smile or a word for each one of them. But then he came to her, and he stopped. She looked at him, the curly brown hair, the cheerful brown eyes, and felt the air of confidence that he seemed to radiate. Dan made everyone feel optimistic.

'Don't tell me—a hard shift,' he said. 'Specially arranged because it's your first day back.'

'They're all hard,' she told him, 'but this one was harder than most. Even the doctors were involved— poor Freddy was up all night. A ventouse extraction.'

'Ah, poor Freddy,' said Dan. 'Did you have a word with him, Midwife McCain?'

'I did. You'll be pleased to know that he enjoyed

Merry Stirling's farewell party, and that he even made a new friend there.'

'You were there?'

'I went just for the presentation and stood at the back. I liked your speech, by the way. I thought you got the mixture of wit and seriousness just right.'

'Well, thank you. And you say Freddy enjoyed himself?'

'He seemed to be. Put it this way, he didn't seem to be suffering from a broken heart.'

'I like to see my junior staff making friends. Let's hope this friendship lasts a while.'

'Freddy certainly seems smitten.' She didn't want to talk about Freddy—she was curious about something else. 'What are you doing here? she asked. 'You're not on duty and there was no emergency when I left.'

'I came to see you. First, because I just wanted to see you, second, to ask if you'd like to come and look at more babies. On Thursday evening, to be exact. I'm going round to see Alice and my nephew and niece. Alice asked if you'd like to come, too. Nothing formal, not a proper meal, but perhaps a cup of tea for an hour before you start your shift.'

'That would be nice,' she said. 'I'd like that. Helen and Stephen are recovered, then?'

'They're well on their way. Are you going to spend an hour in your garden now?'

'Of course, as always. Just for an hour, though. I feel tired.'

'I'd like to come with you—if I were invited—but work is looming.' He paused a minute and then said, 'You're tired, and you don't want a big emotional declaration now. But…I was glad you told me about your…early life.'

'It's over,' she said. 'I've started a new life.'

'Good. Pick you up about seven on Thursday, then?' She saw him glance up and down the corridor. They were now alone. Placing his hands on her shoulders, he bent and quickly kissed her. 'Bye, Midwife McCain.' And he strode off down the corridor.

She didn't feel so tired now. The five-minute meeting with Dan had made her feel happy and had put a spring into her step. She walked across the car park, enjoying the now autumnal sun.

When she had got home, changed, made the mug of tea and pulled up a few weeds, she started to think about Dan. He was a nice man. 'Nice' was an ordinary word, but it suited him. He was no trouble, everybody's friend, she liked his company. But he wasn't as easygoing as most people thought. Under that affable manner was a shrewd brain and a determination to get his own way. And at the moment, getting his own way appeared to involve her. Though he was too astute to push her into anything physical.

She wondered if at last she was coming out of the darkness—then she caught herself. She didn't really need men in her life. They were too much trouble. But Dan was…well, he was just Dan.

She fetched the two candles from her shed and set them up in her arbour again. They were a thoughtful present—from someone who could think and imagine. Someone who had sympathy with her. She wondered if she could get some kind of giant holders for them. They would look better above ground level. Perhaps she could phone William and ask him. But she'd have to be certain that she paid him for them.

Thinking of William, she wondered if he would see more of Gemma. She thought he would. There had been a light in their eyes when they'd left which had suggested that this was a friendship—or love affair—that would blossom. And it was due to her! She smiled to herself. It was good to bring happiness into someone's life. Even if she was interfering a bit. Like Dan is trying to interfere with you? the thought struck her.

She was still dressing upstairs when Dan called for her on Thursday, a little early. Jane let him in, and when Sue finally came down she found him sitting easily in the kitchen, a cup of tea in his hand. She had heard the sound of laughter, so it came as no surprise to find him chatting away happily to Jane and Megan. Jane, of course, would have talked to anyone, but Megan tended to be a bit more reserved and it was unusual to see her talking so animatedly.

Dan stood as Sue came into the kitchen and said, 'If I were a woman I would insist on moving into this house. You're all so organised! There's everything a medical person could want. You make a poor man like me feel unwanted and unnecessary.'

'We can see that you're pining away Dan,' Jane put in. 'You look definitely undernourished.'

They all laughed. Dan was wearing a T-shirt, and the muscles of his arms and shoulders were clearly defined.

'Jane will tell you that I've just been to the choir rehearsal. I need help there, but I'll get it,' he said.

'Sue sings around the house when she thinks no one is listening,' Jane said thoughtfully, 'and she's good. Why don't you join the choir, Sue?'

Sue tensed. She hadn't realised that she had been

overheard. And she knew the suggestion hadn't been malicious on Jane's part, but she wished she hadn't made it. She was about to make some excuse or other when Dan said casually, 'Sue can't sing in the choir. She's already got a job, helping backstage.' Why had he covered up for her?

It was time for them to go. Dan finished his tea and Sue picked up the carrier she had left in the hall. It held two carefully wrapped presents for the children. She knew that to a child unwrapping was as much fun as having the present itself.

'They're a pleasant pair of girls,' Dan said as he helped her into the car. 'Having them is almost like having a family.'

'Not quite. For a start, we have a definite set of rules that we stick to—that means that we can live together easily. We all have our own lives, and although we sometimes do do things together mostly we go our own ways.'

She realised that what she had just said had sounded a bit cold, so she added, 'But I like them both.'

'Sounds a good working relationship. What about men friends?'

'The biggest rule is that no relationship should interfere with the comfort of the other two. No unexpected men in the bathroom first thing in the morning.'

She wanted to change this line of questioning. 'Anyway, how are the children?'

'Much improved. Still upset at missing coming to see you, but they hope you'll invite them again.'

'I certainly will,' she said.

Alice's house was about three miles away, down a little cul-de-sac off a smaller road. 'Handy for the kids to play in,' Dan said. The house was an older semi like her own, but quite a bit larger. There was a Fiesta in the drive and the front garden showed those signs of wear that suggested children played there.

Someone must have been looking out for them because as soon as Dan got out of the car two small figures shot down the drive towards him. 'Uncle Dan!' Sue remembered how they had raced towards their grandfather. Obviously the Webster children never walked when they could run.

Like his father, Dan bent down to pick one up in each arm, and was kissed on each cheek. 'Remember Sue,' he asked. He held Helen and Stephen out towards Sue, and she was kissed on each cheek in turn. She liked it.

'Are you better now?' she asked.

That was a difficult question. After some thought Stephen said, 'Mummy says we are better, but not better enough to go back to nursery. Now, will you come round to the back, please?'

Most of the back garden was obviously the children's preserve, though Sue could see a healthy vegetable garden further down. Nearer, there was a swing, a sandbox and a Wendy house. The lawn was quite worn. Patio doors opened onto a terrace with a wooden table and chairs, and from inside the house she could hear music. Sue thought she recognised the song, recorded by someone who had been quite famous some six or eight years ago. She used to like the song but she couldn't remember the singer's name.

Alice stepped out of the patio doors. 'I see you've been officially greeted. Come and sit down and I'll fetch some tea.' She kissed her brother-in-law, then kissed Sue. 'Helen and Stephen, leave Uncle Dan alone—he needs a rest.'

Carefully, Dan deposited the two children on the ground. 'No trouble,' he said.

'Alice, who's that singing? Sue asked.

'Lee Wright. The song is "Nothing left to Give". Why, d'you like it?'

'I used to. I lost my copy, but the song brought back quite happy memories.'

Helen was peering into the carrier that Sue had put by her chair. 'What's in this bag?' she asked.

Sue took out two shiny parcels and handed one to Helen and one to Stephen.

'I've brought you a little present each because you've been ill.'

'Ooh, thank you! Mummy, can we open them?'

'I've been very conventional,' Sue said as the three adults watched the children pulling at the paper. 'Pink paper for the girl, blue for the boy.'

Dan looked at her thoughtfully. 'Nothing wrong with conventions,' he said. 'Sometimes it's just the best way of doing things.'

She had bought the children a rubber ball each, which tinkled as they were thrown. Stephen threw his up but didn't manage to catch it. Helen did the same. When Alice who had disappeared for a few minutes, came back out with a tray of tea she found Sue and Dan patiently throwing and catching the two balls.

'Come and sit down, you two,' she commanded, 'or you'll be worn out. That pair will have you playing as long as you are willing. Now, I know you're not expecting to be fed, but I did make you a quick sandwich.'

Sue thought it was pleasant, sitting there in the late evening sun. She drank her tea and had a sandwich, but still found she was expected to throw the occasional ball.

'They're thoroughly recovered,' Dan observed.

'Recovered and full of beans. I'll be glad to get them back to nursery school. Sue, I'm sorry we couldn't get to your party.'

'Me, too. But you can come again soon.'

Helen came up to Dan to see what he was eating. She was offered a bite of sandwich and in no time she was sitting in Dan's lap, sharing his food. Stephen saw that he was missing something and soon Sue found that she also had a child in her lap, sharing her sandwich.

'Let Sue and Dan eat in peace,' Alice said mildly. 'You two have had your tea.'

'They're no bother,' Sue said, and Dan nodded his agreement.

In fact, Sue was rather enjoying holding Stephen. 'I'm only used to tiny babies,' she said. 'It's nice to see them a bit older.'

'Wait till you have them twenty-four hours a day,' Alice said darkly.

The garden wasn't quite as well kept as hers, but the presence of children made it…livelier. Yes, it was very pleasant, sitting here in the open air. She wondered if she was missing something, and for a moment she shivered.

Dan spotted it. 'Are you cold?' he asked solicitously. 'There's a bit of a chill now.'

'No, I'm not cold. I just thought…all gardens should have children in them.' The remark slipped out before she could stop it. Dan looked at her thoughtfully.

'Just ask their dad if that's true,' Alice said. 'Whenever he wants to do something they have to help.'

It couldn't have been timed better. At that moment there was the sound of a car from the front of the house. Mickey had just arrived. 'Daddy,' shouted the children, and ran off again. 'It's tiring, just watching them,' Alice said.

First Mickey had to admire and play with the new balls. Then he was allowed to come to the table, kiss his wife and say hello to Sue and Dan. Sue liked the easy relationship between the two brothers. For a while the four chatted, then Alice went inside to fetch more tea and Dan was fetched to play ball.

'It's good to be in the open air,' Mickey said, taking off his leather jacket and slinging it over the back of his chair. 'For the past two hours I've been sitting in a nasty little club that hasn't seen daylight in years.'

'You're in charge of the drugs squad,' Sue said, frozen. 'Don't you...? Is it difficult not bringing your work home with you?'

'Sometimes it's difficult,' he admitted. 'In my job I need to mix with all sorts of unpleasant people. Often it's hard to keep yourself distanced. I've known one or two coppers—mercifully very few—who have have slipped. Either they've been on the take, or they've got into drugs themselves. It's not good. And sometimes just to do the job you've got to be hard on people. There's no fun in leaning on people who are fundamentally weak. But often, if you don't, they'll lean on you. Sometimes I'm scared I might bring home the wrong attitude to my family.'

Sue leaned over and put her hand on his arm. 'You won't do that, I know,' she said. Then she smiled and went on, 'Apart from anything else, Alice wouldn't let you.'

He smiled back. 'It's good to talk to you, Sue,' he said. 'After what I've heard over the past few hours, you restore my faith in humanity.'

'We see some odd examples of humanity in the delivery suite,' she told him. 'My biggest shock when I started was finding out that not only nice people have babies.'

'I can believe that. But I like listening to Dan, talking about his work. I don't think he wants to listen to me.'

At that moment Dan rejoined them. 'I was just telling Sue about how hard a police inspector's life is,' Mickey said lazily. 'She sympathises with me.'

She saw Dan glance at her assessingly, but all he said was, 'We come across a fair number of drug addicts in hospital.'

Shortly afterwards Alice announced that she ought to take the children to bed, and Dan said perhaps he should take Sue home as she was working that night. There was a swift round of farewells, then Sue was in Dan's car again.

'You did know that Mickey was an inspector in charge of the drugs squad?' Dan asked.

'Yes, I knew. I wouldn't want the job myself, but he seems very…balanced.'

'That's a good way of putting it,' Dan said, after a pause.

'I can tell that you two are brothers. But he seems more driven than you.'

'We're both driven. But in different ways.'

'I like seeing you with your family. You're happy

there. And I like Alice very much. She's promised to lend me a couple of CDs.'

'I was Mickey's best man. It was a good day.'

They were turning into her street and she glanced at her wristwatch. 'There's an hour before I have to be at work,' she said. 'Have you got to be anywhere in particular?'

'Nowhere. If you asked me to sit in your arbour for a while, I'd love to do so.'

'You read my mind.'

So they sat there in the dusk. She switched on the little fountain and felt perfectly at peace as she listened to its trickling.

'So how are you enjoying being a real midwife?' Dan asked after a while. 'Being your own boss instead of having to work under somebody else?'

It was a good question but there was no doubt about the answer. 'The responsibility's there,' she said, 'and I'm aware of it. Every now and again we get some weird cases, but the difference is what makes things so interesting. And usually there's a happy ending. Not all medicine can say that.'

'I agree. I always get a kick when I pull a slippery little body into the world.'

'Mmm,' she said. 'As well as all the other things you do. You know, you work too hard.'

He looked complacent. 'I'm having a holiday soon—well, a break anyway. I'm going to the States, to Boston for a conference.'

'You'll not have much of a holiday,' she told him. 'I've heard they work you hard.'

'I shall thrive on it.'

He slid along the bench they were sitting on and put his arm round her shoulders. At first she tensed, and she knew he could feel the rigidity of her muscles under his hand. But he didn't move his arm, and gradually she could feel herself relaxing. It took some doing, but she leaned against him. 'You're good for me,' she told him.

She liked it when he kissed her. He was gentle, holding her with the lightest of touches. If she'd wanted, she could have easily broken away. But she didn't want. She knew he wouldn't hurt her.

Slowly, gradually, his kisses became more intense. She liked it still. But then she wondered about the time. As she eased him away his hand brushed her breast, whether by accident or design she didn't know. What she wasn't prepared for was the lightning flash of excitement that it gave her. She didn't respond this way to men! The shock made her catch her breath.

She managed to look at her watch. 'Time I was going to work,' she said.

He held her two hands in his own. 'All right. We have plenty of time Sue, plenty of time.' They walked back to the house.

Next night they had a house party for Jane's birthday, her twenty-ninth. There were just the three of them, Megan, Jane and herself. Jane had other festivities planned, but they wanted to have a small party on their own.

Sue cooked a chicken curry with a big dish of basmati rice. Meanwhile, Megan carefully made sambals—onions in vinegar, cucumber yoghurt, carrot and raisins, flash fried poppadoms. Perhaps a real Indian would have objected to it, but it was cheap, filling and very enjoyable. There were two bottles of wine and cake on which Sue had laboriously planted twenty-nine candles.

The big joke of the evening was Jane's biological clock. She said she was going to get herself a man before she was thirty or give up trying entirely. 'I shall be a medical old maid,' she sniffed, 'and put the fear of God into all new young doctors.'

It was a good evening, these two being the nearest to a family that Sue had so far, and she enjoyed their company. She went to her evening shift, smiling.

She felt happier than she had in months And the next night everything turned bad.

It was about an hour before she needed to leave for the hospital. Jane and Megan were both out. The door-bell rang and she had a vague feeling of anticipation—could it be Dan? He had told her that he had a meeting that would go on very late, but perhaps he had been wrong.

She opened the door. It wasn't Dan—it was Nigel.

She looked at the figure of her stepbrother in dismay. For three and a half years she had neither seen him nor heard from him, not even a Christmas card. That had suited her fine. A host of unwelcome emotions churned through her breast as she looked at the weak face, the easy, ingratiating smile, which had got him out of trouble so many times. Usually by getting *her* into trouble.

He looked pasty with poor skin. He was dressed in a shabby anorak and jeans and by his feet was a large holdall. Things must be bad, Sue thought. Nigel always used to dress well—somehow.

'What do you want?' she asked. She didn't feel like pretending she was pleased to see him, for she wasn't.

He was a part of the nightmare her life had once been. And Nigel was going to cause trouble. He always did.

'I've just come up north to see my little sister,' he said lightly, ignoring the coldness of his reception. 'I decided to give up the job in London. I wanted to see what opportunities there are up here.'

'There are no job opportunities up here, you should know that, there's too much unemployment. Anyway, what qualifications do you have? And why did you decide to give up the London job?'

Nigel had done something vague in the recording industry. Exactly what, she'd never tried to find out.

'I just thought it a good time to move on,' he said evasively. 'Sue, any chance of a cup of tea? I've only just got off the bus.'

Unwillingly she let him in. She didn't like the way he sprawled on her couch, kicked off his shoes, and said, 'And if you could do me a sandwich as well?' But she got his tea and sandwich.

'I'm going to work soon,' she said. 'I'm on the night shift. Is there anywhere I can drop you off?'

He looked surprised and hurt—he had always been good at that. 'But I thought I could stay here for a while. At least for tonight, just till I get myself sorted.'

'What d'you mean—"sorted"? And you can't stay here tonight. There are just three girls here and we have rules. No men staying overnight.' This was a slight exaggeration, but not much.

'I'm not just any man—I'm your brother, aren't I?' he asked sulkily. 'And I'm not intending to stay too long. Anyway, it's your house, isn't it?'

'It's my house, but I set the rules and I agreed to stick to them.'

'Come on, Sue, you can't throw me out. We've

been through a lot together. First you, me and Ma, then you, me and Doug.'

'Oh, yes. Me, you and the late, unlamented Doug Jones.' Her husband and Nigel had got on so well. They had been soul mates.

It would soon be time for her to leave, and she just didn't have the heart to start a fight. She knew how tenacious Nigel could be when his own comfort was at stake. So she said, 'All right, you can stay in my bed tonight.' She certainly didn't want him in her bed-room, but she couldn't put him on a couch anywhere. She didn't want to upset the other two girls. 'I'll be back early tomorrow morning, and I'll want my sleep, so you'll have to be out of the bed by seven.'

'Sure, sure,' Nigel said. 'Whatever you say, Sue.'

She took him upstairs, remade her own bed with fresh sheets and told him he was not to look in the other girls' bedrooms. Then she left a note in the kitchen for Jane and Megan, explaining the situation. She didn't like the way Nigel was wandering round, picking up odd things, examining them, putting them back. She didn't like his self-satisfied smile.

Just as she was about to leave he asked casually, 'Couldn't let me have a couple of quid till I get to the bank tomorrow, could you, Sue?'

She knew this tactic of old. 'Till you get to the bank? Will there be anything in it when you get there?'

He shrugged. 'Well, you know how it is…'

She gave him a five-pound note. He looked at it and said, 'Come on, Sis…'

'Don't call me that! I'm no sister of yours.'

'All right, all right. But if you could make it a ten-ner…oh, and a key. I'll go out and look for a place.'

As she drove off her last memory was of his self-satisfied face. She knew she was in trouble.

Her mind whirled. It was the sheer surprise of it. If she'd had time to prepare herself, she might have managed better, though somehow she doubted it.

Only by chance did Nigel have her address. Her solicitor must have given it to him some time ago. Certainly, apart from the solicitor, no one else in London had it. The last thing she had expected—the last thing she had wanted—was to find Nigel on her doorstep.

Nigel had always been the delight of his mother—the woman who had married her father. She had never cared for Sue, though she had been careful not to let it show.

Nigel had been the only one to show Sue any kindness. He was charming to everyone—so long as he got his own way. His kindness to Sue had been casual. It had cost him nothing but she'd been grateful to him. At one stage of her life it had been the only kindness she had received.

He had turned up again when she had...when she'd married Doug Jones. Doug and Nigel had been alike. Doug had treated Nigel as a servant, as the man who would do anything. Nigel hadn't minded. He'd fetched drugs for Doug, and both of them had offered drugs to her. Not once had she taken any.

What was she to do? The habit of looking after Nigel, of letting him get away with things, was so firmly engrained in her that she wondered if she would be able to break it.

Fortunately she had an easy shift. In fact, for the first few hours she had nothing to do but answer one midwife's call to come and take the baby. Perhaps it was a good thing—she couldn't concentrate. She drank coffee, walked the corridors, tried not to brood.

At about half past eleven she met Dan. He came, smiling, down the corridor towards her, dressed in the dark suit, white shirt and college tie that showed he had been in a meeting. Six hours ago she would have been pleased to see him, but now…she just wished he had stayed away. He couldn't help her.

'How's my favourite midwife? I need to see a happy smile because I'm disgruntled. I've just come out of a meeting with fifteen of the finest minds in the hospital. It took us five hours to decide what any one of could have done in twenty minutes.'

Before she realised what he was doing, he had pulled her into a corner and kissed her. Ordinarily she would have been delighted, but now she had too much on her mind. It was typical of Dan that he sensed something was wrong at once.

'Problems?' he asked, still holding her. 'Anything wrong in the delivery suite?'

She shook her head and listlessly twisted out of his grasp. 'Everything's fine here—in fact, it's a very quiet night. I've just had a bit of a…surprise, I suppose.'

'Obviously not a very happy one. Tell Dan about it. Problems solved at a minute's notice. At the very least, the very best quality of sympathetic ears lent.'

'I'm sorry, Dan, you can't solve this problem. I appreciate your offer of help, I really do, but, please don't push me. I'm under enough strain already.'

He stood back, frowning. 'Of course I won't push you, it's the last thing I want to do. But, Sue, all troubles are better shared. Let me try to help—I really want to.'

But there was no way she could tell him about Nigel. It would expose too much of her past, and she didn't even want to think about it herself.

'Sorry, Dan. Like I said, this is something I must deal with myself. Once again, I appreciate your offer but there's nothing you can do. It's not a lot really. Now I've got to go, I've got things to do.'

She stepped back into the corridor and walked rapidly away. But she knew she hadn't fooled him. Dan was too shrewd.

CHAPTER FIVE

THE kitchen was in a mess when Sue got home. There were dirty plates on the table, food stuck to the bottom of the frying-pan, drawers and cupboards left open. Food that wasn't hers had been taken out of the fridge, used and the remainder left to thaw. There was no way she could have her usual hour's gardening.

She knew that neither Jane nor Megan would have done this. It must have been Nigel who had come in after they had gone to bed. Angrily, she set to to bring some kind of order to the place. There was no way her two friends were coming down to find this!

After making herself a drink, she went upstairs, threw open the curtains and then shook the motionless lump on the bed. Nigel wasn't pleased at being woken. 'What time d'you call this? I'm tired. Can't you wait a while? Sue what are you—?'

She pulled the pillow from under his head, then shook him again. 'I've just done a ten-hour shift. I told you when I'd be back. Now get up.'

'OK, OK, I hear you. I'll be down in ten minutes.' He frowned at her. 'Any chance of a cup of tea?'

'Yes, there's one in the pot downstairs.'

'What I meant was—'

'I know exactly what you meant. Now get that body of yours downstairs!'

It was half an hour before he came down. 'I'm not used to rising this early,' he said. 'D'you know what time I got in? It was—'

'I'm not interested. Now, I've done you a sandwich. Take it and get out before my two friends get up. And thanks for the mess you left in the kitchen.'

'You can't expect me to get out now! Where will I go?'

'I'm not only expecting, I'm insisting. Go and find that job you're looking for, and somewhere to live as well.' She kicked the bag he had left on the kitchen floor. 'And take your bag with you.'

It took another fifteen minutes of arguing, cajoling and persuading before he finally went. He persuaded her to let him leave the bag, saying he would collect it later. 'If you're going to sleep all day, how about I borrow your car, Sue? You're not going to need it.'

'Borrow my car? No chance! Besides, you're still banned, aren't you? Now get out so I can have my sleep.'

She saw him out. This was a nightmare. Somehow she managed to finish tidying up before her two friends appeared. Then she went to bed herself, but had difficulty sleeping. Too late she remembered that Nigel still had a key.

He was downstairs when she woke. She woke early, a rare thing for her. Usually she slept well. But there was the sound of the TV downstairs. It was too loud, which was most unusual. The three of them were careful not to waken anyone who might be sleeping.

When she opened the bedroom door there was an odd smell to the place. Downstairs the kitchen was in a mess again, there were papers all over and the remains of a meal on a tray. Slouched again on the couch was Nigel. She should have known.

'What are you doing here? I thought you were looking for a job, looking for a place to sleep?'

'Be cool, sister, it takes time to get sorted. I'll get a job in time.'

'You've got one now.' She moved over and switched off the television. 'The kitchen's a mess like it was this morning. I'm not your slave—you get up and clean it.'

'I was watching that programme! I'll do the kitchen in a minute.' He moved to switch on the television again but she stood in his way.

'You'll do the kitchen now. My friends are due back shortly.'

It had always been like this. Nigel needed constant pushing to do anything. It was so wearing that in time it was often easier to do the job yourself. But not this time.

'Look, sis,' he said, trying the ingratiating smile, 'why don't we—?'

'I told you not to call me that. I'm not your sister. Get in that kitchen.'

Reluctantly, supervised by her, he started to clean up. He finished by squirting far too much washing-up liquid into the bowl. She sighed. She knew he'd done it on purpose.

The doorbell rang. Wondering what more could happen to ruin her day, she went to answer it. It had better not be someone trying to sell her something!

It wasn't. She didn't like the way the expensive black car had reversed into her drive, preventing anything from getting in or out. And she certainly didn't like the man who was waiting politely on her step.

She couldn't tell exactly why. He was about forty. His clothes were obviously expensive and he looked excessively well groomed. But the slicked, spiky, blond hair didn't go with the dark, shiny suit. His pink shirt—probably silk—didn't match his unpleasant tie. He looked hard. There was something menacing about the set of his shoulders, and when he smiled his eyes remained cold. But his voice was courteous enough.

'Hello, I'm looking for Nigel. My name is Tony Sellars. Nigel is a friend of mine.'

'I didn't know Nigel had friends up here,' Sue said flatly.

'We met quite recently. We have mutual acquaintances in London.'

Sue really didn't want him in the house, but somehow he was there in the hall and then walked into the kitchen. 'Hello, Nigel.'

The voice was still courteous but the effect on Nigel was tremendous. 'Hel-hello, Tony,' he managed to quaver.

Sue knew Nigel of old. He was terrified. Sometimes he did something wrong, and there was just no way that his charm could put it right. This was one of those times. 'How did you manage to find me here?' he eventually managed to say. 'I was coming to see you later on.'

'I'm sure you were. But I have a lot of friends. You were seen coming in here, so I thought I'd drop in and give you a lift.'

Nigel looked to Sue for support. 'Tony might… might find me a job,' he said.

'That's very good,' Sue said. 'How could Nigel help you, Mr Sellars? What exactly do you do?'

The man waved his hand vaguely. 'I'm a business-man, I have a lot of interests. Clubs, shops, some property. I import fruit and so on from abroad. What do you do, Miss…?'

'My sister's a midwife,' Nigel burst in. 'She works in Emmy's—you know, the big women's hospital.'

'That must be very interesting. I'm always pleased to meet people who work in hospitals. Rewarding work, I'm sure—even if not well paid.'

The words were innocent enough. In fact, she agreed with everything he said. But there seemed to be an edge of menace underneath. She couldn't understand it.

'Tony and me, we're just going out,' Nigel put in quickly. 'Tony, I'll just get my coat. We'll talk about that job—I'm sure I can do it. Get in the car. I'll be right with you.'

There was silence as Tony looked calmly from Nigel to Sue, and she wondered how such an act could appear so threatening. 'Of course,' Tony said suavely. 'Nice to have met you, Miss McCain. I'll only keep Nigel for a couple of hours. I'm sure we'll meet again.'

Not if I can help it, she thought as Nigel escorted the man to the door, but she said nothing.

The door closed and Nigel rushed back. 'Sue! Lend me some more money!' She thought she had never seen him look so desperate.

'What for? I told you, I'm not going to—'

'Sue, lend it to me! Please! I promise I'll pay it back. It's just that I...I've got to have it.'

She went upstairs, took fifty pounds out of its hiding place. 'That's the last,' she told him. 'Just don't bother asking again.'

His expression of gratitude made her feel sick. She knew he thought he had won. 'Thanks, sis! You're a sport!' He ran out of the door.

It was starting again. She sat down in the kitchen,

her head in her hands, wondering what to do. There was this pressure, the force of years. She just couldn't ultimately say no to Nigel. She could bully him, make him work, but she couldn't throw him out. And he was in real trouble now. She didn't know how or what, but she knew that Tony Sellars was bad news. And Nigel would drag her down into any trouble he was in.

The doorbell rang again, giving her an even bigger shock. Surely they weren't back! She couldn't stand it. She did something she had never done before—crept into the living room and peered through the curtains. Then she heaved a sigh of relief. It was Mickey. But what was he doing here?

When she opened the door he offered her a small parcel. 'Hi, Sue. Just a flying visit. Alice sent these two CDs round. She says to keep them as long as you want. Apparently you liked them—they're by Lee Wright.'

Confused, she accepted the packet. That pleasant evening in the garden was only three days ago. It seemed so long ago! Somehow she managed to mutter her thanks. Then, with an effort, she gathered strength from somewhere and asked, 'Would you like to come in?'

He smiled. 'I'm afraid I haven't time—busy as always.' Then he said something that afterwards struck her as rather odd. 'Alice and I dote on Stephen and Helen, you know. We'd do a lot for the midwife who brought them into the world.'

'That was Gemma, not me.'

'Alice remembers you as being very supportive, very concerned. Anyway, hope to see you again soon.' He turned and walked down the path.

There was just too much to cope with. She put the CDs on the kitchen table and waited for her churning thoughts to settle. Then she thought about Mickey. There had been a blandness about him she had not met before. His manner had been different from when they'd been in the garden together. Perhaps because he was—presumably—at work.

The answer to emotional problems was physical work. She would turn over the kitchen—it needed a spring-clean. But before she did, she found an air-freshener and ran round, spraying everywhere and opening the windows. She recognised the odd smell now. She remembered it.

Half an hour later her phone rang. For a while she sat and looked at it. It didn't stop ringing. Problems didn't disappear if you ignored them. She picked it up.

'This is your favourite specialist registrar,' a friendly voice said.

She wouldn't have thought it possible that she wouldn't want to hear that voice. But she didn't. She felt she couldn't cope. 'Hi, Dan,' she said weakly. 'Nice of you to phone.'

'I'm coming round,' he said. 'We've got things to talk about. I'll be about half an hour.'

He couldn't come round! No, she had to be by herself. She faltered, 'I...I've got things to do, Dan. I'd like to see you, but right now it's just not...convenient.'

'I didn't ask you if I could come round, I told you I was going to.' His voice was still friendly, but there was a new tone in it. She had always known Dan could be tough. Now it was coming out.

'But, Dan, I—'

'Half an hour!' Then his voice grew gentler. 'You

know I…and other people…think a lot of you. Put the kettle on. I'm on my way.'

That was it. She sat at the kitchen table. She hadn't done it for over four years, but she wept.

When the bell rang again she didn't have the heart to do anything but answer. She knew she must look a wreck but she didn't care. So what if her hair was all over, her face blotched, her eyes red? If Dan wanted to interfere, he must see her as she was.

She felt a mess. He stood there in his formal clothes, obviously fresh from the hospital. But he'd taken his tie off. As if he was ready for work.

He stepped inside and closed the door. She could say nothing, but stood, looking at him. He wrapped his arms round her and hugged her to him. It wasn't a sexual hug—well, not very—but it was so, so comforting. For perhaps five minutes they stood there without speaking, and the conviction grew in her that perhaps things weren't too bad. 'I feel better now,' she said. 'You can let me go. Anyway, how did you know I was—?'

He released her, offered her his handkerchief. 'I bet you didn't put the kettle on,' he said. 'Never mind, I'll do it myself. Here, sit in the living room, and I'll fetch us both a mug of tea.'

Obediently, she did as he told her. It was good to stop thinking, to let someone else do the worrying, make the decisions. When he returned with the tea she drank half of it, then cast about wildly for something to say to him. There was no need though, as he spoke first.

'You're in more trouble than you can deal with,' he said flatly. 'Mickey phoned me half an hour ago. He said that when he called here he smelled marihuana.

That's something. But, more important, he saw a man leave your house who he knows is a local drug dealer. A really big dealer, and he's into all sorts of other unpleasant things. Mickey recognised the car, and pulled in to see what was happening. So now you're to tell me what's going on.'

She knew she didn't have to tell him. For so long she had kept her own counsel, worked out her own destiny. She had trusted no one, especially no man. But now she wanted to confide in Dan. It felt good to talk to someone, to share in her misery.

'Well,' she said, 'it's Nigel, my stepbrother. He just appeared. I haven't seen or heard from him in nearly four years. You remember how I told you that my father remarried, and the woman he married had a son already? Well, that's Nigel.' She told him about the odd relationship they had, how, because he had once shown her a few odd acts of kindness, she was now incapable of standing up to him.

'I know he's weak and idle.' She said. 'I know his faults all too well. He and my ex-husband were well suited—they got on very well. And now, when I thought I'd finally got rid of my old life, he's moving back in and he thinks he can batten on me again.'

'Oh, I don't think so,' said Dan quietly. 'If he wants to move back into your life, we'll have to show him that he can't. You know I once worked with an oncologist—a cancer specialist. He told me that, after trying chemotherapy and radiation, sometimes the only option was surgery. Then you had to be ruthless and cut out everything that was diseased. Otherwise the patient would die.'

She realised then how angry he was. And, like many quiet men, he was fearsome when angry.

'Please, don't hurt him,' she begged. 'He's not really bad, just weak. It's probably the result of having that mother—she thought he could do no wrong.'

'But he *can* do wrong,' Dan answered. 'Don't worry, we'll try to ensure that no harm comes to him—so long as he stops hurting you, that is. Now, d'you start your shift at nine-thirty as usual?'

'No. It's the beginning of my rest period.' She looked at her watch, amazed. It was only four o'clock 'How did you get out of work,' she asked him. 'Haven't you got a clinic this afternoon?'

'I did have. I got the junior registrar to take it. I'm an important person, I can get other people to do my work. Now, will Nigel be back?'

'Oh, yes. Nigel will be back all right. He'll always be back while he thinks he can get away with things.'

'I guessed so. Now, I have a couple of calls to make on my mobile—how would you like to make me a sandwich? Cheese would be good.'

'All right,' she said. She was going to leave everything to him—not bother, not worry. With the decision the sense of pressure she'd felt disappeared. It felt good. Just for a moment she wondered why she had let Dan take over so easily.

She made them both a sandwich and more tea. Then she sat by him on the couch, and he put his arm round her shoulders, letting her rest against him. She had slept badly and had got up too early, and she was tired. It was comforting to doze against Dan, knowing that he would take care of everything.

An hour later there was another visitor—or, rather, the same one again. She opened the door to let Mickey in. Sue saw the glint of anger in his eye, and there was something about the way he held his body that showed tenseness. But he smiled at her reassuringly. She was glad his anger wasn't directed at her. She suspected he could be fearsome, like Dan.

To her surprise he leaned forward and kissed her gently on the cheek. 'It's all going to be all right,' he told her. 'This is my business. I deal with cases like this all the time. You'd be surprised at the number of innocent people who get caught up in drugs.'

They went into the living room. Mickey grinned at his brother. 'Why don't you stick to helping babies get born?' he said. 'Don't you think I don't have enough to do?'

'I doubt it,' Dan replied happily. 'I pay my taxes so that my brother can work twenty-five hours a day like me. Now, if you smile at Sue, she might fetch you a cup of tea.'

Sue shook her head and went into the kitchen. One Webster brother was bad enough, two was almost an avalanche. She felt that once they'd decided on something, nothing could stand in their way.

She still had to do her little bit for her stepbrother. 'I hope you're not going to be too rough on Nigel,' she said. 'I know I might be wrong—but I don't think he's too bad. Just weak.'

'I've been in touch with London about him,' Mickey said. 'They know him there. He's weak, like you say, but has never been vicious. He's never had anything to do with violence, for a start.'

'No,' Sue said, 'he wouldn't.'

'And he's right out of his league, trying to deal with Tony Sellars.'

Mickey apparently didn't want to say any more about the subject. He turned to Dan and asked, 'So how's the show going?'

'Well, very well,' Dan said amiably. 'We've got a good choir, we've got some semi-professional acts and there's a man who is willing to act as stage manager. Thank God I don't have to do that. And I've just heard that we can have the Lanston Theatre for less than cost. We're going to make some money. Do you know it, Sue?'

She blinked at him. She was having difficulty jumping from her problems with Nigel to a consideration of stages, acts and theatres. But Dan had asked her a question and she would answer it.

'I know the Lanston Theatre,' she said. 'I've been to a couple of shows there. It's lovely inside.'

'It's got state-of-the-art lighting and acoustics,' Dan said. 'And we've persuaded a lot of the backstage men to work free.'

'How did you do that?' Sue asked curiously, knowing that backstage workers weren't the most sentimental of people.

Dan winked. 'Many of them have wives who have had, or are going to have, babies. I tell them that it's in their interests to help. I'm trying the same blackmail on newspapers and an advertising agency. We're going to turn a profit!'

Mickey turned to Sue. 'Sometimes I think I ought to lock him up. He's more unscrupulous than a lot of crooks I know. He'll use anyone, even you or me, if he thinks we can help him.'

'I hate myself sometimes,' Dan said, completely deadpan. 'The things I find myself doing.'

She liked being with these two. There was their obvious regard for each other, the gentle joking. And they included her. When she was with them it was like being part of a family.

Half an hour later there was the sound of a key in the lock. She knew it wouldn't be Megan or Jane as it was too early. It had to be Nigel.

'We'll talk in here,' Mickey said. I want you both with me but, Sue, Dan, this is my business. Don't interfere. Don't say anything unless I ask you to. Don't answer his questions.'

There it was again—it must be a family trait. There was no raising of the voice, but a very clear indication of who was in charge.

'We won't interfere,' Dan promised, 'will we, Sue?' She shook her head.

'Hi, sister,' Nigel shouted from the hall. His voice was slightly slurred, and there was a confidence in his voice that told her he had been taking something. He went on, 'There are two cars outside. Have you been...?' He opened the living-room door and looked surprised at the two men sitting with Sue.

Dan stared at him expressionlessly. Mickey stood slowly. 'My name is Inspector Webster. I am a police officer. Here is my warrant card.' He flipped open a leather wallet, then returned it to his pocket. 'I am in charge of the drugs squad in this city.'

Nigel looked round wildly, his previous mood having disappeared. 'Sue, you've turned me in,' he wailed. 'Why did you have to—?'

'Shut up,' snapped Mickey. 'We've been following your associates for quite a while. Now, turn out your pockets.'

'I don't have to—' started Nigel.

'You have to do what I say. Either here or at the station—I don't mind.'

Nigel looked round for help, but there was none. Sue kept her gaze firmly on the floor. Reluctantly, he piled up the contents of his pockets on the coffee-table. Mickey picked up the wallet and opened it. Inside was just one five-pound note. Sue wondered what had happened to the money she had lent—given—him.

'Right,' said Mickey, 'sit down and keep quiet. We've got waiting to do.' He sat down himself. Irresolute, Nigel stayed erect. 'I said sit down! Mickey rasped. 'And I also said keep quiet. Remember that.' Nigel collapsed into a chair.

It was hard for Sue to sit there, saying nothing. She carefully avoided Nigel's eye, but she knew it was harder for him. Dan and Mickey appeared to be unmoved by the silence.

After about ten minutes Nigel just couldn't keep silent any longer. 'I say, Sue, I'm thirsty. I don't suppose you could—'

'Keep quiet!' Mickey only spoke softly, but Nigel obeyed at once.

More minutes trickled by, then Mickey's mobile phone rang. As the others watched him, he answered. 'Good…good. Is he?… Get him his solicitor, it'll save time.… Tell the lads that it's a job well done, there'll be a drink on me.… I'll be there in half an hour. I might have another one with me.'

With what seemed like extreme care he put his phone away. Then he turned to look at Nigel and leaned forward. 'My men have just picked up Tony Sellars. We caught him with the drugs on him. I'm going to the station to interview him now.'

Nigel was white-faced. 'Nothing to do with me,' he said. 'He was supposed to be offering me a job. I only met him a couple of days ago.'

'Try telling that to the judge.' Mickey settled himself comfortably in his chair, and Sue thought she had never seen such a sadistic smile. 'The thing is, Nigel, Tony is very angry. He can't understand how he came to be picked up. Now, I'm going to interview him shortly. You've been interviewed at a police station, I know. You know what it's like—you have to give a little to get a little. So I may give him a little. I may tell him that you're the one who provided us with the information. You know what that will mean, don't you?'

'But I didn't give you information! I said nothing to you! You can't tell him that!' Sue felt pity for Nigel now—his terror was so obvious. She wanted to intercede to tell Mickey that Nigel wasn't really bad and what he was suggesting was wrong. But she didn't. She remembered what she had been told, and kept silent.

'You can tell him you didn't give me information,' Mickey said silkily. 'Do you think he'll believe you?'

'But…you can't… I haven't…' Nigel was now beyond words.

'Perhaps I won't have to,' Mickey said. 'Quite frankly, I don't want you on my patch. I'd be glad to see the back of you. There's a train to London in half an hour. I could drop you at the station if you like. If you're on that train, I see no need for your name to come up.'

'I'll go,' said Nigel, 'only don't say anything to Tony Sellars.'

'I'm sure I won't have to.' Mickey surveyed the shaking form of Nigel a moment longer, then took a card out of his pocket. He gave the card to Nigel. 'This is the address of a place in London. It's had some success with people like you—finding them jobs, a place to live, helping them get clean. It's the opposite end of the city from where you were…operating before. If you don't want to spend the rest of your life running from the likes of Tony Sellars, you should give it a chance.'

Nigel took the card. 'Just don't come back to my city as an addict,' Mickey said. 'In fact, don't come back at all.'

Five minutes later Mickey led Nigel out to his car. Before he did so Sue pressed fifty pounds into his hand. 'To pay for his train ticket,' she whispered, 'and a bit more.' Mickey nodded curtly.

Sue stood looking out of the window, watching Mickey's car drive away. 'A busy afternoon,' Dan said.

CHAPTER SIX

SUE couldn't move. When the car had driven off she slumped back in her chair and stared unseeingly at the wall. It wasn't like her. Usually she was tough, could make her own decisions. But she had handed over to somebody else, seen her problems sorted out with a ruthlessness she could only gasp at.

Dan seemed to understand. After a while he said, 'It's still warm out. Why don't I make us yet more tea and we can go to sit in your arbour? I'd like that.'

'So would I,' she said. 'But I'll make the tea. Leave me something.' Somehow she forced herself to stand.

'Are the girls coming back later?'

It took her a while to work out what he meant. She replied, 'No, tonight they'll both be away.' It often happened that way. Megan visited her parents, and Jane often staying the night with friends. She went on, 'And I'm starting my rest period. I was going to do some gardening…and all sorts of things.'

'You still can—now,' he said.

She made the tea, put it on a tray and he carried it down the garden for her. Together they sat on the bench in her arbour and drank tea. She had flicked on the water pump, and the little fountain trickled softly. There were the other sounds she knew and loved, the rustling of leaves, the occasional call of a bird. There was still the faint smell of flowers, though soon it would be gone. But the sharpness of the eucalyptus trees was still evident. Despite her ever-present awareness of Dan, Sue found herself relaxing.

'It's always peaceful here,' Dan said.

'Yes. I always used to come here for some peace, but I came alone. Of course, Jane and Megan would come down sometimes, and we'd sit and chatter, but I used to look forward to my own company. I'd sit here and get my thoughts together. But...I can find peace here with you. I've never said that to any other man.'

He didn't reply, but leaned over to stroke her hair. Then he moved closer to her, and she clung to him. The feel of him was wonderful, calm and peaceful, but subtly charged with strength and sensuality.

He reached for her hand. She disengaged his fingers and said, 'Don't hold my hand, hold my wrist. Be a doctor—tell me what my pulse shows.'

He did as she'd directed. 'It's slowing,' he said. 'I know it was up before, but it's slowing now. Midwife McCain, have I ever told you what a perfect pulse you have? Firm strong and steady. It would bring joy to the heart of any doctor.'

'Thank you, sir,' she said. 'That is a compliment I shall never forget.' He was a lovely man to be with.

After a while she said, 'I feel a lot better now. You're good for me, Dan. You know when to say nothing. I like that.'

'Not a common quality in doctors, but I know what you mean. In future I shall cultivate the impressive silence instead of the verbose explanation.'

She giggled. 'I don't think you are the impressive silence sort of man.'

'You never know. In fact, there have been times when I thought I was communicating better by keeping silent with a two-hour-old baby than I was talking to its mother.'

'Now, that feeling I do know.' She smiled. 'All this talk about silence—it's made me want to talk.'

He waved elaborately. 'Talk away. In line with your wishes, I shall say nothing.'

'You're an idiot! There are things I need to get settled in my mind. Now, I like Alice no end and I think she's very lucky. And I like Mickey. But I didn't realise he could be so…well, so hard. And he's your brother. Are you a bit like that?'

He thought a minute. 'First of all, I hope I can be if necessary. It's not exactly being hard, it's a willingness to do what has to be done. You know sometimes doctors have to make decisions. Do I risk the mother's life to give the baby a slightly bigger chance? What about the husband, possibly other children—what does the mother herself want? Sometimes you can consult, ask other people. But too often you have to make a split-second decision. And it's important that you do decide. Just waiting to see what will happen is to opt out of your doctor's responsibility. Now, Mickey does what he has to do. Sometimes he appears hard. But it's only because he believes implicitly that what he's doing is good.'

'He certainly shocked Nigel, didn't he?'

Dan's face altered, grew sterner. 'Nigel needed a shock. And it's not impossible that some day he'll be grateful to Mickey.'

There was a pause while she thought about this, and then Dan laughed. 'I'll tell you something that perhaps I shouldn't. He's my brother so I've known him a long time. Mickey could have been a great actor. He played Hotspur in the school play and he was magnificent. In fact, they won some kind of schools drama competition. Sometimes I wonder if he's still playing Hotspur.'

'He certainly convinced me.'

Dan squeezed her. 'Don't worry, he'll have a friendly eye kept on Nigel, even in London. There is a gentler side to Mickey, but don't tell him I said so.'

He glanced at his watch. 'I'll have to go soon. I managed to get rid of most of this afternoon's work, but in another half-hour I'm due at the theatre. I've got this director chap, Max Morgan, organizing all the acts. He says we have to meet on the stage.'

'Your fault for taking on so much,' she told him.

'Don't I know it. There are always problems with people. Ticket-sellers, printers, insurance policies and, above all, artistes. I ask you, artistes! Not artists but artistes with an ''e''. We've got some really good acts, but do they create! Worse than surgeons in the theatre. D'you know, one even screamed at me because I said Mac—'

'The Scottish play,' Sue chipped in quickly. 'Don't laugh, Dan. They do it because they're frightened. Everyone is before they get on stage. Once on it…no trouble.'

'Yes,' he said slowly, 'that makes sense. How did you know that?'

'Read it, I expect,' she said lightly. 'Dan, I don't want to stay on my own tonight. Can I come with you to the theatre? If I won't be in the way.'

'I'd love you to come—after all, you promised to help backstage. But not singing?'

'Not singing,' she agreed. 'I couldn't go on stage. Give me a minute. I want to change into something, well, nicer.'

She felt she had been in jeans and sweater for too long. For a change she wanted to feel feminine. They walked back to the house, and Dan sat in the kitchen while Sue rushed upstairs. It only took a minute for her to have a lightning-fast shower. Then there was a dab of her favorite scent, frillier underwear than normal, a dark green dress that did much for her figure and colouring.

He was a bit surprised and obviously impressed. But she was reassured that he controlled the banked heat in his eyes. 'You dress up too seldom, Midwife McCain,' he said. 'When you do look wonderful—as you are doing now.'

'After today I felt the need to dress up,' she said.

Sue loved the Lanston Theatre. It was in the centre of town, but there was ample parking or it was easy to get there by public transport. It had been built at the turn of the century, and somehow managed to battle on, without being turned into a cinema or bingo hall. Inside it was ornate, painted in gold, red and cream, with elaborate plasterwork and varnished mahogany. There were boxes, balconies, a bar on each floor, and everything was well maintained. She loved it.

When she met him she loved Max Morgan, too, from the centre-parted hair past the pink bow-tie to the patent-leather boots. Max was in his fifties—late fifties. With his fast, shrill voice and his ever-gesticulating arms, he was a complete contrast to Dan. But she saw very quickly that Max knew what he was doing. He was a professional—his behavior was an act.

'Old Hitchcock had it right, dear,' he called to Dan. 'Treat your actors like cattle. This lot are quite amenable, and I've more or less got them licked into shape. This is a show I'm pleased to be associated with—you must have had a tongue of silver to get them all. but we still need a top of the bill! You promised me you'd get someone more or less big.'

'I've got a lot of feelers out,' Said Dan. 'Anyone in the theatre whose wife has ever been treated at Emmy's has been written to. I've tried all my pals in London. Don't worry, someone will turn up.'

'I hope so.' Max sniffed. 'Who's this lovely creature, then?'

'This is Midwife Sue McCain,' said Dan. 'She wants to work backstage and I thought you might like her as your gopher.'

'She looks strong,' said Max. 'Can you carry gin in that bag, dear?'

Sue was surprised. 'D'you allow alcohol backstage?'

'On the day—or days—of the show, you'd better have some just for me. Keep it in a cough-mixture bottle. Now, Dan, these musicians you've got...'

It was dark when they had finished. Max turned down the offer of a drink, and Dan and Sue stood outside the theatre, watching him walk away. 'He'll be good,' said Sue positively. 'He's got the feel, knows his stuff. You picked well there, Dan.'

'I rather suspect he picked me. I must admit, he worried me at first. He's not a...hospital-type person. But you say he'll be all right?'

'Well, I should think so,' she said hurriedly backing off. 'Of course, I know nothing about it.'

He looked at her in silence for a moment. 'It was good of you to come round with me,' he said. 'I know you were working last night—how d'you feel now? Tired?'

'Quite the opposite. In fact, I should just be starting my shift just now. But such a lot has happened over the past twenty-four hours, Nigel appearing and then going so quickly. I can't believe my luck. I thought it would take me weeks to get rid of him. Does that sound callous?'

'Not at all. But if you're not tired…'

'If you're about to offer to buy me a drink, then the answer is, yes, please, I'd love one.'

'Great. And how long since you ate?'

She blinked. 'Now you mention it, it's ages. I think I'm ravenous. I need food. Why do all doctors, nurses, midwives have such awful eating habits?'

'It goes with the job,' he said. 'I remember one fantastically busy six-week period when I calculated that over half the calories I took in came from Mars Bars. But I've learned better since then.'

He looked around. 'We're in the city centre here, we've got time to ourselves and we don't need to be in tomorrow morning. Let's dine in style and comfort. Within five minutes' walk there are Chinese, Indian, Korean, Greek, Spanish and Mexican restaurants.' He paused and added casually, 'There's even a pub where they do English food. Great food. But you choose.'

'Don't let anyone ever call you inscrutable,' she told him. 'Take me to this pub—that's where you want to go.'

'You guessed,' he said.

He led her to a back-street business district that she knew would be heaving in the middle of the day but which was less crowded in the evening. There they had a bottle of red wine and a typical pub meal—beef in beer with chips and salad on the side. And it was wonderful! 'They don't buy stuff in ready-made,' Dan told her. 'it's all made on the premises.'

She just managed to finish the meal. Then she looked at him and said, 'I feel better than I have in quite a while. You're good for me, Dan. Everything we do together I enjoy.'

'So do I,' he said quietly. 'Shall we have coffee?'

It took her a long time to answer, but eventually she said, 'If you take me home now I'll make you one there. Or if you want I'll take a taxi home—it is getting late.'

'Don't be silly,' he said. 'And I'd love a coffee at home with you.'

Both were quiet on the journey home, and as there was little traffic they were back quite quickly. She led him to the kitchen and started the coffee percolator. From the depths of a cupboard she took a bottle and dusted it. 'I've never opened this,' she said. 'I don't drink whisky. Would you like some?'

He took the bottle from her and whistled silently. 'The Laphroaig. This is the king of whiskies. Where did you get it?'

She smiled. 'It was given me by a grateful new father. He was so happy that I didn't have the heart to tell him I didn't drink spirits.'

'It's good to have happy parents,' he agreed. Both of them knew that not every baby came into the world loved and wanted.

They sat each side of the kitchen table, talking casually about medicine, gardens, places they had visited. She realised he was tired, too, so made him pour himself another whisky, and then another. He only poured very small measures, she noticed. There was something intimate about sitting there with him. Usually if she sat, talking, in the kitchen, it was with Megan and Jane.

She couldn't help it. She yawned. He noticed and said, 'It's time I went. You must be shattered.'

She didn't reply. When he stood she said, 'Sit down. I don't want to be left on my own. I don't want you to go. I want you to stay with me. Can you…? Do you want to?'

There was a silence, then he replied. 'Yes, I'd like to stay. I think perhaps I've had a little too much to drink. I was going to phone for a taxi. But if I could stay on your couch or something…?'

It was a decision she wanted to make herself. She could feel the moment pressing on her, needed to say the words, but somehow it was so hard. The silence dragged on and then, somehow, she managed to say, 'I want you to stay in my bed.'

Her head was still bowed. She felt his hand reach across the table and take her chin to lift her head so he could look into her eyes. Tears blurred her eyes, but she could still see into his. They were brown, like her own. They were kind eyes. This man could never be cruel to her.

He read her thoughts. 'I will never hurt you Sue,' he whispered. 'I know you have been hurt before, but I will never hurt you.'

'I know that,' she said swiftly, 'I know that if I know nothing else.'

He sat there as she put the cups into the sink, then with deliberation flicked off the light. The two of them were now shadows, only the light from the hall out-lining them. 'Come to my bed,' she said, and held out her hand.

He waited a minute then took the proffered hand. Pulling her to him, he took her face in both his hands, then stooped and with infinite delicacy bent forward to kiss her. For a while their only contact was his hands on her face and their lips. At first it was the sweetest of kisses. But then she found her heart pumping, her breath coming faster. She slipped her arms round him, squeezed hard, his kiss deepened and became more passionate. She knew he shared her feelings. His breath, too, was ragged and she thought she could feel the beating of his heart through his shirt.

His hands dropped and his arms wrapped round her. Then he put his hands on her shoulders and moved away. 'Sue…?' he asked. The single word meant so much.

She knew what he was doing. He wanted her to be certain. He was giving her a chance to back away. But she didn't want that chance. 'Come upstairs,' she said.

She had hated having to leave Nigel in her bedroom. It was like her arbour, a place where she could be safe, alone, cocooned. There was a variety of lights and she switched on the bedside lamp, which had a heavy red shade. The room was in half-darkness, looking mysterious, inviting. Dan stood, looking at her.

Because she so often had to work shifts, the room was as far as possible soundproof. The windows were double glazed, the floor heavily carpeted, the door had a thick blanket hanging behind it.

She had bought herself a double bed. At one time she used to thrash about in her sleep. On more occasions than one she had woken terrified, sweating, wrapped in bedclothes in a heap on the floor. It didn't happen so often these days. Perhaps she was learning.

There were extra pillows on the bed so she could

sit up and read, a small TV so she could watch if she wanted and a bookcase by the bedhead. She had never envisaged bringing a man here. She had wanted so much for Dan to be with her, but now it seemed as if she didn't quite know what to do with him.

He looked round, walked to touch the heavy curtains, scanned the titles of the books by her bed. 'You feel safe here,' he said. 'I recognized the feeling at once. It's a comforting room.'

She had to make him see what she was trying to do. 'It's not an escape,' she told him. 'It's a retreat. I love my work, I think that I'm good at it. But there are times when I need to be…by myself.'

He nodded slowly. 'I understand,' he said, and she knew he did.

She turned her back on him, lifted her hair at the back and asked him to undo the catch on the thin gold chain round her neck. It was an old, much-loved chain, but sometimes the catch was difficult. He had deft fingers and the catch was loosened in a trice. It was an intimate little act, and made them seem close again. The touch of his fingertips on the sensitive skin on the back of her neck made her shiver.

All her senses seemed heightened. When he dropped the chain on her dressing-table, she heard it rattle. There was a pause, then he took the fastener of the zip on her dress and drew it slowly downwards, from the nape of her neck to her hips. Once again the tiny buzz seemed louder, more significant.

She was still standing with her back to him. She felt his fingers pull the dress across her shoulders and slide along her arms as he gently eased the dress downwards. She wondered if he would turn her, but he didn't. There was no way she could turn herself. He was in charge.

Now his lips touched the back of her neck, that incredibly erotic line at the top of her spine, and moved along across her shoulder to the top of her arm. And he held her so gently, loosely clasping the insides of her elbows, where the pulse was beating. She leaned backwards a little to tell him how much pleasure he was giving her.

Her breathing was heavy again, and she could feel a warmth creeping across her front. She rocked backwards against him, to press against his body. He moved his hands, there was a momentary tightness and then he had undone her bra. The little scrap of white lace fluttered downwards. 'Stay there,' he muttered, and she did as she was told.

He released her and stepped backwards. There was the rustling of clothing, then he eased her against him again. This time she leaned against the warmth of flesh, her nakedness against the heat and smoothness of his skin instead of the roughness of his shirt. His arms were round her again, clasping her breasts, stroking her gently, then fingering, teasing, till her nipples peaked with excitement. And she could tell he was aroused.

She clutched his hands and pulled them harder against her. And all this time he was kissing her back, her neck, her shoulders. This was so wonderful! They stayed locked there together for what seemed an eternity, she thought. But perhaps it was only a few minutes.

She kicked off her shoes. Perhaps this suggested something to him. His hands left her breasts, stroked downwards. He felt the concavity of her waist, then his fingers were on the waistband of her briefs, pushing them down so they made a froth of whiteness round her ankles.

She kicked them away. Now she was naked, now she felt free.

His hands slipped further round and she gave a little gasp of surprise as his fingers brushed excitingly against the curliness of hair. Then he moved. One arm slipped round her knees, the other round her shoulders and she was lifted, swept upwards. He cradled her in his arms for a moment, and she saw the darkness burning in his eyes as he bent his head to kiss her. He was strong!

He took two strides to the bed, and lowered her onto it gently. Then he lay down beside her. She rolled over to look at him, a being of muscles and shadows. His body was warm. There was a hint of muskiness of cologne, and underlying it the infinitely thrilling scent of maleness.

Now it was her turn and she reached out to him. Slowly she ran her hand over the muscles of his chest and shoulders, felt the beating of his heart in the powerful column of his neck. Her hand strayed lower and she thrilled as he gasped when she touched him.

His thigh crossed hers as he took her head between his hands and kissed her, not gently as before, but harder, demanding, expressing his need for her. A need she now shared. She pulled him to her, thrust her breast against his chest, opened her mouth to the onslaught of his tongue.

Their need for each other was now so strong that she thought she could smell it in the air. When she took her mouth from his and kissed his neck, his chest, she thought she could taste the maleness. She knew she, too, was warm. The heat of her body in turn was making her smell of desire.

Now he was above her. For a moment she opened her eyes to see the passion, the yearning in his. She reached to kiss him one more time, then opened herself to him. He was so gentle. She revelled in having him, holding him. But she needed more, she needed release. Surely he did, too? She surged against him.

Her life—the past day, the past year, the past six years—now seemed a wasteland of foolishness that only he and only now could put right. Her body responded to his, to their growing desire, moving together as one until both called aloud at a moment of climax that seemed almost unendurable in its ecstasy.

They lay there side by side, the warmth of their bodies cooling, her neck cradled in his arm. She ran her finger across his lips. 'You make me so happy,' she said. 'Now I want to sleep.'

'You made me happy, too,' he told her. 'Sue, I…we…'

'No talking,' she told him. 'No talking. Just be and enjoy. You can stay the night with me?'

'Yes, I can stay the night. But I must be at work tomorrow. You're not at work?'

'No. Now sleep.'

She slept well. Once or twice she woke, found his arm round her or heard the sound of his deep breathing so she knew he was there by her. Then she slept again.

Sue was wakened by him in the morning, switching on the bedside light. With the curtains drawn, even in daylight it was always dark in her bedroom. Dan leaned over to kiss her as her eyes blinked open. 'Morning, sweetheart. I've brought you a mug of tea.'

She wriggled up in bed to look at him. Since she had slept without her pyjamas, this revealed her breasts, and she pulled at the sheet to cover herself. Then she gave up the struggle. After the events of the previous night, it was a bit pointless. And anyway…she didn't mind.

He was damp. There was a towel wrapped round his waist and droplets of water sparkled in his hair and on his chest. 'I made myself at home,' he said. 'I pinched this towel, and even had a shave with a lady razor—that was a nasty experience.'

'You have my sympathy,' she said. 'When d'you have to be at work?'

He shrugged. 'I should leave in about half an hour.'

'You've got yourself some tea?' He had a mug in his hand. 'You must think me a terrible hostess. I should have been up and making you breakfast. In fact—'

'Don't you dare offer! All I ever have is tea.'

'I wasn't going to offer you breakfast,' she said demurely. 'I was going to invite you back into bed.' She reached out, grabbed the edge of the towel and tugged. 'I'm naked. You can be, too.' she said, throwing the towel on the floor. 'You know, you do look nice.'

She was still warm from sleep, his body was cool. She pulled him to her anyway. 'You're cold,' she said, 'and it's lovely.'

For a while they lay there, just holding each other. Then he struggled to sit up. 'Drink your tea,' he said sternly, 'and listen. We've got to talk. Last night was—'

She interrupted him. 'Last night was wonderful. I don't want you apologizing or anything silly like that.'

He looked indignant. 'Me apologise? For last night? Never! I was going to ask when we could do it again.'

'Now?' she teased.

'I'll have to drink my tea first. But...' He put his hand on her breast.

She took his hand and held it there for a moment. Then she put it away. There were things she had to tell him. 'Listen, Dan, there's something I have to say to you. I told you I was married, that it was lousy and I guessed it messed me up a lot. Well, you—and last night—convinced me that not everything, not everyone is as bad as I thought. I don't know what I mean to you and I don't know what you're going to mean to me. But I...like you a lot. You've showed me things that I hadn't thought possible. You're kind and gentle and....and—it's an exact word—you're a wonderful lover. You came to me with love, and I'll always be grateful for that.'

His face was serious. 'You're laying ghosts, aren't you, Sue? You're working your way through your past life, trying to break out of it.'

'Something like that. My ex-husband is dead, and I'm glad. But I still have to come to terms with what he did to me.'

He took her hand. 'I want to help, I really do. Because I think I—'

'Don't say it!' she warned, almost panicking. 'Don't say that you...love me. If that's what you were going to say. It was said to me before, so often, and then he turned out to be... And I just don't like anyone saying it. For me, it's always a lie.'

'It doesn't have to be,' he told her quietly. 'For many people it's the centre of their lives. They say it and for them it's true. But I know what you mean. So for now I'll just say that you mean more to me than any woman I've ever known. Now give me a hug!'

She did. Then they both drank their tea. 'Sitting her with you is so nice,' he said, 'but there are nasty things coming. You know I'm going away for a few days? To Boston?'

She had forgotten! 'A conference,' she said. 'Yes, you did tell me.'

'I'll miss you. Will you miss me?'

'Yes, I'll miss you a lot. But in some ways it will be good for me. I can think about things, sort of get used to the idea of having you around. Will you phone me?'

'Do you want me to?' He looked down and said, 'That seems to be an odd question to ask a lady whose breast I am currently holding.'

She laughed and leaned over to kiss him. 'Yes, I certainly do want you to phone me. Now, did you say you had to go to work?'

'I should be there,' he said. 'Paperwork mostly. I've left a lot for young Freddy to do, but I don't want to overface him. I'm not on the ward, there are no clinics. I just want to make sure that all goes well while I'm away. I want to see Max Morgan, too. Incidentally, if you want to act as his gopher, will you phone him to confirm it?'

'I do want and I will phone him,' she said.

'Good.' Dan looked at her with an odd expression. 'Of course,' he said, 'I could arrive a bit late. It wouldn't really matter. I wonder what could delay me for half an hour?'

'I wonder, too,' she said as his lips came down to meet hers.

* * *

Sue always enjoyed her breaks. Because she worked long hours on nights, and often worked through the weekends, too, when her breaks came they were quite lengthy. Usually she worked in her garden, caught up on her reading, studied a little.

She offered to run Dan to the airport, but there were a few others going from the north-west and they'd arranged to travel in a special minibus together. So she pottered round the house, doing the odd chores that always seemed to crop up. But she was happier than normal. There was a smile on her face. No longer did she dread the long periods when there seemed to be nothing to do. Now there was plenty that needed doing.

She phoned Max and went round to the Lanston Theatre to see him. With there being so many acts, there were a lot of detailed arrangements to be made—deciding where people should go, working on dressing rooms, looking at lighting plans, negotiating with the head electrician.

Once or twice Max was surprised at the suggestions she made. 'Anyone would think you'd done this before,' he said. 'You know what the flies are, what front of house is, what jellies are.'

'I'm just a natural-born busy-body,' she told him. 'Now, there's going to be a big gap here unless we…'

She thought a lot about Dan—and then decided not to think about him. Or, rather, not to think about what future they might have. She didn't want to think about the future. Just so long as she could stop being haunted by the past. There were things still that Dan didn't know about her, and she couldn't work out just how to tell him. It was all so hard. So she would think about the present.

She did that a lot, and when she thought about him she always smiled. He was such a good man. She could shut her eyes and conjure his image up, the sound of his voice, the feel of his hair and his skin under her palm, the smell of him, half cologne, half himself. Dan was with her every minute she cared to think about him.

He phoned her after a few days and his voice was as clear as if he had been in the next room. 'They had a tea party here some years ago,' he said, 'and threw all the English tea in the harbour. And they haven't made a decent cup of tea since. Are you missing me?'

She wondered if he could tell what she was feeling over the telephone, if it could transmit emotions as well as sounds. 'Actually, yes, I am missing you. I miss that man bringing me tea in bed in the morning.'

'Good. I'm also missing you, but I'm learning a lot. Did you know that…?' After that the conversation was pleasant but light-hearted. Like her, he obviously felt that the telephone wasn't a good medium for really intimate conversations. So they chatted for a while, and when he rang off she felt much happier.

Next day Mickey turned up to see her. This time he did come in for a drink, and they sat, talking, in her living room. She was pleased to see him. It gave her an odd thrill, to be with a man who looked and sounded so much like Dan and who yet wasn't him.

'I wanted to talk a bit about Nigel,' he said after a while. 'You did realise I was bluffing when I threatened to tell Tony Sellars about him?'

'I wondered,' she said. 'You were very convincing,'

'Good. It's not the way I would choose to behave, but when the end is a good one sometimes you have to.'

'I understand. I've had some experience with drug addicts, I know you can't reason with them. And as for drug dealers, I'd hang them!'

He looked at her, surprised at her anger. 'You feel strongly about it,' he said.

She shrugged and tried to laugh it off. 'Just my little hobby-horse. A lot of nurses and midwives feel the same way. Anyway, what about Nigel?'

'I heard from London this morning. With some extra coercion Nigel went to the place I suggested, and signed on the programme, if a bit reluctantly. Rachel—my contact down there—said that although he's only been there for a few days, she thinks he'll stick it. Apparently the first few days are often the hardest.'

'Good. So, by chasing him down to London, you did what was best for him?'

'I'd like to think so,' he said. 'Certainly it's better than hanging round with Sellars's mob.'

'This place he's gone to. Is it a charity? Will they accept donations? I'd like to give some money. Could you send it?'

'I could if you wanted. They're always short of cash.'

She fetched her cheque-book, wrote out a cheque and gave it to him. He glanced at the amount and looked surprised. 'You've made a mistake. You don't want to give this much.'

'I do,' she told him, 'and I can afford it. I hope it does some good. Now, when Dan comes back I hope you'll all come round for tea. I want to see Alice again.'

'Yes, Alice will phone you in a day or two. In

fact...' Mickey blushed '...she wants a bit of profes-sional advice. Just a chat at first.'

Sue guessed at once what he meant. 'Another baby! Mickey, how lovely. How long gone is she?'

'Only about three months, I think.'

'Well, we'd better get things organized. But since this will be number three she'll know what to do her-self. Does she want me to help her deliver? I could probably pull a few strings to make sure I was the midwife. But some women prefer to be seen by a stranger.'

'Not Alice,' he assured her. 'She wants someone she knows.

Sue had a problem in he garden. Right at the back, behind her arbour, there were a few old apple trees. They didn't give much fruit, but she'd never got round to cutting them down and she liked what they did pro-duce. Now she decided they were in trouble. There was a white fan of fungus under the bark at the base of each tree, and round them were spotted a set of toadstools. She needed expert advice—she knew fun-gus could do incalculable damage to a garden.

She could have phoned William, but she decided to go and visit him instead. She rather fancied a chat with him. Grabbing a cardboard box, she put in samples of toadstool and fungus. Then she set off for the garden centre.

'I'm a friend of Mr Webster,' she told a young lad when she arrived. 'If he's not too busy, I'd like a word with him.'

He took her to the greenhouse she had visited be-fore. Opening the door, he shouted, 'Mr Webster! Another visitor for you.' Then he pointed to the far end of the greenhouse and said, 'Go through that door, miss.'

Before she got to the door it opened and William appeared, smiling. 'Sue! Good to see you. Come on in, there's a friend of yours here.' She walked through the door and there was Gemma, blushing slightly.

William was dressed as he had been before, in the comfortable clothes that were suitable for working in the greenhouse. Gemma was dressed smartly in a light brown dress that enhanced her figure and a touch more make-up than normal. 'It's good to see you two as well,' Sue said. 'Look, this is just a flying visit. I want a bit of professional advice.' She had decided very quickly that she wanted to leave these two alone.

'Have you time for a cup of tea?' William asked. 'Gemma has been baking and brought some scones.'

'I'd love a drink. But could I first peep at your new flowers? How are they coming on?'

William was only too pleased to show her his new plants. 'Coming on quite nicely,' he said, stroking the leaves. 'I'm going to enter this one for the competition. I've got hopes of first prize.'

'What are you going to call it?' she asked, looked at the bright-flowered plant.

'I don't know yet. There are lots of possibilities. Now, before we got to get that tea, what's your problem?'

She opened the cardboard box. 'I've a couple of old apple trees in the back. And I've just found this fungus under the bark, and toadstools as well.'

William peered and frowned. 'Honey fungus,' he said. 'It's nasty, it can spread. The trees are old, you say?'

'Very old, I think. I don't get much fruit from them.'

'Cut them down. Burn the trees and the roots, and treat the ground with Armillatox. I've got some in the centre—I'll give you some. But be careful what you plant afterwards. I'll give you a list of things that honey fungus won't touch.'

'That's great! And I'll buy this Armillatox stuff. William, this is your living. I've got to pay for it.'

'All right,' he said amiably, 'but you can have it at trade price. Now, let's go and get that tea.'

He wouldn't let either Gemma or Sue into his kitchen. 'You sit there,' he said. 'I'll be along with a tray in a minute.' The two were left alone.

'I didn't expect to see you here,' Sue said with a twinkle in her eye. 'Or perhaps I did.'

'I've seen a lot of him recently,' Gemma confessed. 'Nearly every day, in fact. He's a lovely man. I've got to thank you for bringing us together, Sue. You did it on purpose, didn't you?'

'Well,' said Sue, 'I did wonder if you'd...like each other. But I thought I might be interfering.'

'I wish more people like you would interfere. I don't know why, but before I just couldn't take myself out. I didn't want to meet other people. I'm still reasonable-looking, I've still got...feelings. Once or twice I've been asked out but I've always said no. Now I wonder why. You saw something that I didn't, Sue.'

William entered at that moment with the tea and scones. The scones were as good as he'd said. They talked for ten minutes longer, then Sue left, saying she had to call in at the hospital. That wasn't quite true, but she wanted to leave the couple alone.

As she drove home she found herself oddly happy. She had made a lot of new friends recently—William, Alice, Mickey, the two children, Dan. Dan, of course, was different. Then she realised they were a family. For the first time in her life she was joining a family. She'd never had one before—not a real one. Her early life had been a misery and for the past five years she had kept strictly to herself.

Then another thought struck her. Families didn't have secrets from each other. That wasn't so good.

CHAPTER SEVEN

NEXT morning Sue was wakened by Jane. That wasn't normal—usually the girls left each other to rise when they pleased. And she was starting her night shift later. But things weren't normal. 'Read this,' Jane said, standing at her bedside. 'Just read this.' She pushed a newspaper into Sue's hands.

'I don't normally read the Sunday papers before I've got up,' Sue said, yawning. 'In fact, normally I don't read this at all.'

'Today is different. The newsagent told me about it when I called this morning. Look at page seven.'

Wondering what the fuss was all about, Sue did as she was told. Then her face blanched as she read the headline. Consultant Gets Two Salaries—But Only Does One Job. And underneath was a picture of Megan, her friend. 'Junior doctor tells all,' read the caption.

Sue knew that there had been gossip in the hospital about Charles Grant-Liffley, one of the consultants, but she didn't know it had got into the papers. And what had Megan to do with it? 'I'm sure she knows nothing about this,' Jane said, 'and she's not going to like it.'

Sue was reading the article. In its way it was clever. Very little was actually stated, but the hints and suggestions were there for everyone to think about. 'We'd better wake Megan up,' she said. 'She's going to need all the help she can get.' Sue's voice was bitter. She didn't like papers like this one.

* * *

In some ways it was good to be starting work again. Each shift was different—there was always something new. Sue drifted along to handover that night, chatting to midwife Jo Colls.

'We have a change tonight,' Sister Reeves said after she had allocated all the jobs. 'Because we're rather short of doctors, we've got a locum in from…another hospital, I think. Dr Tanner will be the junior registrar for a while. That'll be all.'

The words were fine, but the intonation was not. Sister Reeves obviously didn't like Dr Tanner. 'Wonder what he's done wrong to upset Sister?' Jo whispered to Sue.

'No idea. But he's certainly not winning any popularity prizes.' Sue dismissed the problem. 'I wonder what this new mum I've got is like?'

Her patient was Leonie Fletcher, a primigravida. She was in the first stage of labour and had been for some considerable time. The birth should be straightforward. There was no partner with her—apparently he was a soldier, abroad—but Leonie was said to be a good patient. The only slight grounds for worry was the length of time the baby was taking—but probably it wouldn't be serious.

As ever, after introducing herself, Sue had a little chat. She wanted to feel out the patient's attitude to the baby, find out how the father was coping, ask where the new family was going to live. She found that a little bit of early friendliness helped her patients to relax. And it was important that, even though she saw so many, the women should be individuals and not merely cases.

Leonie was coming along well. Sue had just filled in the latest reading on the partogram when she heard the door behind her open and a male voice said, 'Hello, who have we here?'

She took against the voice at once. It was self-satisfied, ingratiating. She turned to see a white-coated figure, presumably Dr Tanner. He was aged about forty and had an expression that matched the self-satisfied tone of his voice. He sported what Sue thought was a silly little moustache. And the minute she saw his smile she knew he was going to be trouble.

There were a lot fewer doctors about now who thought that the female staff were just there for their pleasure, but there were still a few. Sue knew at once that Dr Tanner was going to be one of that number.

'This is Leonie Fletcher, Doctor,' she said. 'Coming along quite nicely and we hope to see something soon.'

Dr Tanner didn't say anything to Leonie, which Sue thought unforgivable. Instead, he said, 'I came to see you, actually,' he said. 'Anything I can do for you?'

'No. Everything seems to be in order.'

He came over and stood close to her, much closer than was necessary. She realised that he had recently been smoking—his white coat stank of tobacco. She stepped back and picked up the partogram pad so there was something she could hold between them. 'Do you wish to examine the patient, Doctor?' she asked. She hoped he didn't. She wanted to spare Leonie that.

'No. I'd like a word with you, though—in private. When d'you expect to have a coffee-break?'

'I don't know. We'll have to see how things go.'

'Well, I'll be around and I'll drop in to see you now and again. It's been boring so far. It's nice to see a pretty face around.' Obviously certain of his own charm, Dr Tanner walked out.

Leonie said, 'I don't want him anywhere close to me, Sue. The smell nearly made me sick. I've always hated the smell of tobacco. Ooh!'

'I'll get you some Entonox,' Sue said.

After a while Leonie settled down and Sue felt able to slip out for a while and get some much-needed coffee. No matter how she prepared for it, the first shift back on nights was always tiring. She sat in a chair, sipped the coffee and closed her eyes. When she opened them there in front of her, like a bad dream, was Dr Tanner.

'It's the pretty midwife, McCain,' he said 'I've been hearing about you. People say you never go out with anyone.'

'Haven't you got anything better to do than listen to hospital gossip?'

Dr Tanner was too insensitive to be brushed off. 'Ooh, ooh,' he said. 'Pretty midwife has a tart tongue. I just wondered what you were doing later. I thought you might like to go out—for a drink or something. Or you could come round to my room. I've got a place here in hospital and I always have a couple of bottles handy. We could have a nightcap at the end of the shift—a sort of morning cap.'

Was he serious? Sue looked at him disbelievingly and decided that, yes, he was. 'No, thank you,' she said curtly.

'Oh, come on now. You're not married, not seeing anybody. What's wrong with a drink with me? I'll see you at the end of the shift.' He appeared to think a moment. 'If you want, we could go to your place.'

Occasionally she put up with joking that she found a little offensive in the interests of harmony. But there was a limit to what she was willing to put up with, and Dr Tanner was now well across that limit. She crashed down her coffee and stood to face him. 'Dr Tanner, we have to work together, co-operate medically in the interests of our patients. Other than that I want nothing whatsoever to do with you. Now, is that clear or shall I fetch someone to explain it to you?'

He stood, white-faced, in front of her, his mouth working but no words coming out. 'Just who d'you think you are?' he asked eventually. 'Who d'you think you are to speak to me like that?'

'I'm a midwife. We may have to work together, but that is all.' She refused to sit and stared him down. Finally, he turned and slammed through the door. She went back to Leonie.

At about three in the morning things began to go wrong. The monitor attached to Leonie indicated that the baby was showing signs of foetal distress. The baseline was dropping. Sue began to feel alarmed. She performed another internal, and there, over the baby's head, she could feel fingers and part of an arm. That would slow the baby's progress down the birth canal. She didn't want to, but she rang the bell that summoned the doctor.

Of course, it was Dr Tanner. And he hadn't forgiven her. 'What is it?' he snapped. 'Not another pointless call? I was just trying to get some sleep.'

Sue glanced at Leonie and pulled Dr Tanner out of earshot. 'The baby's showing signs of distress,' she said, 'and is presenting part of the hand and wrist.'

He went over, grunted perfunctorily at Leonie, examined the partogram and the monitor. Sue stood by Leonie's head and held her hand as the doctor gave her a quick internal examination. 'Signs are a bit high,' he said to Sue, 'but I don't think there's any need to worry yet. And quite often the hand will slip back into place as the birth takes place. I gather you've just qualified. You'll learn the trade in time.'

Sue took a breath and thought rapidly over what she had been taught. 'I disagree,' she said. 'I think a section might be advisable.'

Dr Tanner couldn't believe he was being contradicted. 'I'm the doctor. I decide if a section is needed,' he said. 'You're just the midwife.'

The door opened and Sister Reeves came in. Afterwards, Sue was to wonder why, but Sister was just who she needed. 'Dr Tanner and I are having a difference of opinion,' Sue said. 'I think my patient may need surgical intervention. I'm not happy about the baby presenting with its arm over its face.'

Sister Reeves turned to look at the monitor, made her own deft examination, then said without any emotion, 'In this room the midwife makes the decisions. If she believes the patient needs further care, she sends for it. Do you wish to send for the consultant, Midwife McCain?'

'Yes,' said Sue. 'I do.'

'I must say I agree with you. I'll have him paged at once.'

Dr Tanner left the room.

Sue had seldom seen the consultant. He was only in at present because Dan was away. But he and Sister Reeves were obviously old friends. He gave Sue a friendly smile, then talked comfortingly to Leonie. A quick scrutiny of the monitor and the partogram, followed by an internal examination, and then he said to Leonie, 'There's no real need for worry, but I'm just going to be extra careful and suggest you have a Caesarean section. We're just a little concerned about the way your baby is lying. We'd like him—or her—out quickly.'

'Whatever you think best, Doctor,' Leonie groaned. 'I've got confidence in you...and the midwife . But I'm awfully tired.'

'Then we'll move quickly.'

The team all knew what to do, there was the usual slick organisation and before very long Sue was watching as a perfect little boy was lifted out of his mother's abdomen.

'Good job. Well done, everybody,' the surgeon said genially. He turned to the paediatrician. 'How's the child, Chris?'

'Well, we'll incubate him for a while, but I think he's healthy. Glad you didn't wait, though.'

The consultant turned to Sue. 'Well spotted, my dear. It was a hard decision—but you made the right one.'

'Thank you, sir,' Sue muttered. 'I'd better finish these forms.' After each birth there was always the same strict procedure to be followed.

As she drove home she wished that either Dan or Freddy had been on duty with her the night before then there would have been no trouble. She smiled as she thought of the problems she'd thought she'd had with Freddy. A few days ago he had said to her ruefully, 'D'you know, I asked Dan to come and plead my case to you?'

'Yes, I know. He told me. But he did plead your cause—and very convincing he was.'

'Not convincing enough. Still, I'm enjoying working with him. Good luck to him—and to you. You've got a good man there.'

She grinned at him. 'Do I take it from your good humour that you have also got a good woman? Thinking of settling down?'

'Midwife McCain,' he said in horror, 'what sort of man d'you think I am?'

By the third night on duty she had settled into her routine. She saw no more of Dr Tanner as he had been switched to a day shift. No one quite knew why, or who had organised it, but Sue did hear Sister Reeves muttering something about 'causing less trouble there'.

The third night was very quiet—so quiet that a couple of the midwives managed a sleep. Sometimes it happened like that. Babies finally made their way into the world when they felt like it, paying no attention to the thoughts or wishes of other people.

Sue walked down the corridor next morning, pleasantly tired but still looking forward to half an hour in her garden. And there, walking towards her, was Dan.

She hadn't been expecting him till the next day. And she certainly wasn't expecting the sudden rush of happiness and excitement that seemed to grip her by the throat and make her incapable of speech or action.

It was only a few days since she had seen him last, but she felt as if she were seeing him for the first time. He felt…new. He was dressed casually, swinging a travel bag in one hand. Closer up he appeared tired and there were little lines by his eyes. But his gorgeous smile was the same as ever.

'Have you missed me?' he asked.

She found she could speak. 'Yes,' she said, 'quite a lot. Have you missed me?'

'You know I have.' There was no one else in the corridor. He kissed her and it was blissful.

After a while she pushed him gently away. 'Mind my reputation,' she said. 'It's a bit early to be kissing someone so passionately. How come you're back so early?'

'I decided to catch the overnight plane and I arrived in Manchester a couple of hours ago. My body clock is now completely messed up. But it's good to see you.'

She didn't need to think for long. 'Would you like to come home for breakfast?' she asked. 'The girls are there, but we could work round them. Or do you want to shower or shave or something?'

'Breakfast would be wonderful. I had a plastic meal on the plane and I could do with something real. And I want to see the garden again.'

'Let's go, then.' She had him to herself—it was what she wanted.

When they arrived at Sue's house, almost automatically she led him to the kitchen and made him the ritual mug of tea. Then they walked together down the garden to her arbour. It was getting much cooler now, but they were sheltered from the breeze. They sat side by side on the bench, and when he put his arm round her she snuggled against him.

'I thought about you, Sue,' he said. 'I thought about you a lot. In some ways perhaps it was a good thing for us to be apart after…after that last night. Even though I did miss you. But I had time to think, to try to come to some conclusions about us.'

'Why d'you have to think?' she asked fretfully. 'Why can't you just be happy with me?'

'I am happy with you. But I want to be…happier.'

Her arms were round his waist and she squeezed him. 'At the moment I'm happy the way things are,'

she said. 'I want to carry on like this. We
were…hurried before, and it was largely my fault.'
She giggled. 'Fault? What a word for it. But I need
time. I've been hurt before and it's hard for me to risk
things again. Like I said, I need time.'

'A good medical principle,' he said judiciously.
'But don't leave it too long.'

'I'll make you breakfast when the girls have gone
to work,' she said, then added with a blush, 'I'm going
to bed soon. Would you like…? That is, you could
stay for a while. If you wanted.'

'I did come back early,' he said. 'I'm not due to
start work till tomorrow. Yes, I'd like to stay.' He
kissed her again.

For some time now there had been distant sounds
from the kitchen—the radio and the rattle of cups and
plates. Megan and Jane were up. Then suddenly there
came the sound of a loud cough, quite close. 'Knock,
knock,' a voice called. 'I'm coming in.' Jane appeared,
in uniform, carrying a tray. 'Two coffees, two large
pieces of toast,' she announced with a big grin. 'I've
brought breakfast for our gardeners. We're going to
work now. Good morning.' And she was gone.

Sue blushed. 'They must be pleased that you're
back,' she said. 'They've never done that before.'

'With a cheerful smile Dan said, 'And what about
your reputation?'

'They won't talk. The girls are good to me. But you
can't count on the rest of the hospital.'

'You can't keep secrets in a hospital,' he said plac-
idly.

'Do you mind? Before I met you I would have said
I minded desperately. People laughing and joking and
teasing and so on. But I'm not so sure now.'

'I don't mind. In fact, I'm happy and I'm proud. If people think that I'm seeing you, they'll envy me. And I like that.'

She squeezed him again. 'I think that's one of the nicest things anyone's ever said to me.'

'And I've no doubt you'll cope,' he went on. 'I had ten minutes in the hospital before you came off shift. I caught up on the gossip. I gather you had a run-in with God's gift to women, Dr Tanner.'

'I coped,' she said. 'I can always cope with dross like that.'

He looked at her oddly. 'You look sweet,' he said. 'Most of the time you are sweet, but there's something tough about you.'

She didn't want to talk about it. 'You forget I was married to a creep,' she said, 'and one who took drugs. I learned to survive from him.' She wanted to change the subject. 'Anyway, what about Tanner?'

Now it was Dan's turn to look tough. 'He's a disgrace to the medical profession. But so far he's not done anything really wrong. But ours is a small world, and slowly he'll find that he can't get a job, that people just don't want him. Doctors are supposed to look after their own. They can also punish them, too.'

From the front of the house they heard the sound of two cars leaving. 'We've got the house to ourselves now,' Sue said. 'If you've finished your coffee we could go...'

'Yes, let's go to bed,' he said.

Both were tired. They made love slowly, gently, happily. It was different, but it was as good as before. Only when he tried to speak to her did she pull him closer and close his mouth with a kiss. 'Don't talk,' she whispered. 'Not yet.'

*　　*　　*

It was rather nice being officially—as one of her friends put it—an item. However, she still intended to stick to the strict rules that they had set about men friends in the house. Just because it was her house, she didn't intend to change. She wouldn't have Dan sleeping in the house while the other two were there.

Jane and Megan tried to make it easier for her. 'I don't mind if he's here,' Megan said, 'I think he's a lovely man.' But Sue wouldn't change her mind, and she hoped Dan didn't mind.

Together they visited William, and found Gemma with him. They admired the flowers and had more tea. Then they visited Alice, and agreed that Sue would be her midwife—it should be possible to arrange—and Gemma would try to come in as well. She liked going to places with Dan.

'Are you two free next Friday night?' asked Alice. 'Mickey has promised to be off early, I've got a babysitter and I thought we might drive out into Cheshire and have a meal and a drink. There's a pub we know by a canal.'

Sue glanced at Dan and nodded. 'Love to,' they both said.

'Good,' said Alice. 'I'll drive, because I've stopped drinking all alcohol, so you three can indulge yourselves a little.'

'But—' Dan started to protest.

'Don't fuss! I'm only about three and a half months gone. I need a bit of independence. Tell him I'm right, Sue.'

'Absolutely right,' Sue agreed. 'Pregnant women shouldn't cosset themselves too much.'

'I see I'm outvoted. Incidentally, who's babysitting?' Dan's grin suggested that he might already have guessed.

'Gemma. She gets on really well with the kids.'

Dan's grin broadened. 'Are you sure she's trust-worthy? You know these babysitters. The minute you're out of the house, the boyfriend calls round.'

'Yes, William is coming as well,' Alice said se-renely. 'But he's all right. I know his family.'

It was a good evening. They drove into the coun-tryside and headed for the pub. It was now too cold to sit outside, but they found seats by a log fire and had a pleasant meal. Then they just sat, talking. Sue felt very relaxed. For a while she talked to Mickey, and found out for certain that the hardness he could show was only a front. And he agreed with her as well. Dan disliked drugs, but Mickey hated them with the same fervour that she had.

It struck her again that this was what having a fam-ily was like. They all were at ease, relaxed, confident in each other's support. There were no secrets among them. She frowned. She wasn't a full family mem-ber—yet. But for the moment she was enjoying her-self. She was taking things easy.

Dan spent more and more time on the show. There was a vast amount of paperwork, phoning and visiting to do. He had recruited a lot of good acts, but so far still hadn't quite got the top-of-the-bill act he was looking for. 'I want it to go right,' he told Sue. 'There are one or two acts that would do at a pinch, but I want someone exceptional. I'll get somebody eventu-ally.' In the past the show had been a more slapdash affair, but Dan was being more professional. It should earn a lot of money.

She regularly went to see Max, and knew he was coming to rely on her. She knew, probably better than Dan, just how much work there was backstage. She noted down Max's shouted thoughts and instructions, typed them out on her PC and gave them back to him. He thought that was marvellous. To Sue, accustomed to writing down at once every drug administered, every process, every observation made, it was second nature.

He was standing in the top gallery one day, looking down on her on the stage. 'You look good there, darling,' he shouted to her. 'You look the part.'

She gave a little curtsey. 'Thank you, kind sir,' she called.

'Now, get up to that microphone and sing.'

'Sing?' She hadn't expected that. 'Sing what? I can't sing.'

'Of course you can. Everyone can sing. I just want you to shout down the microphone so I can test the setting. Sing "Baa baa, black sheep" if you like.'

'No, I can't…'

'Come on,' the exasperated voice yelled. 'There's only us to hear, and it's just like saying, "Testing, one, two, three, four".'

It was hard, but she sang what he had suggested. 'Baa baa, black sheep'.

'You've got a wonderful voice for nursery rhymes. You should be in the choir.'

'No,' she said flatly.

'Suit yourself. Now move to the far side of the stage and try the microphone there.'

It was very nearly December.

She sat with Dan in the hospital canteen, having a

light evening snack before she started her shift. It was a good canteen. The management thought it a definite investment, and subsidised it.

'Max says you're very useful and helpful.' Dan beamed at her. 'He says you have more than a brain—you've got flair. Not the kind of thing he'd expect in a midwife.'

'He's obsessive,' Sue replied cautiously. 'I just tell him what he wants to hear.'

'So you say. Now, we'll get this show out of the way, and then there's Christmas. I'm going to have a real family Christmas and I'd like you to share in it, be part of it.'

'The last two years I was training. But I volunteered to work on Christmas Day and New Year's Eve,' she told him. 'But I won't this year. I'll change.'

'I'm hoping there'll be lots of changes in your life next year,' he told her. 'For a start, why not come off full-time nights? I could see more of you then. I know you'd still have to work shifts, but we'd be together more.'

'All right,' she said. 'Perhaps after Christmas.'

'We'll celebrate. I'll fetch you another cup of tea.'

When he had left, she frowned. She could guess what he had in mind for Christmas. He wanted their relationship to go on further. She wasn't sure she was ready yet. For any relationship involved trust—and honesty. And there wasn't honesty between them yet. she knew it was her fault. But as yet she…couldn't.

It happened shortly afterwards, when she had jut finished her set of nights. She was looking forward to seeing more of Dan when he phoned her unexpectedly. 'Come to the hospital canteen at lunchtime. I want you to meet someone. Share in my good luck. You're going to be really pleased.'

She was intrigued. 'Come on, tell me who it is,' she said. 'I hate secrets.'

'No, it's to be a surprise. Can you make one o'clock?'

She was carried away with his excitement. His enthusiasm was one of the things that endeared him to her. 'OK, I'll be there.'

'You'll really be pleased, Sue. I am.' He rang off.

She walked through the foyer of Emmy's, winked at the gloomy-looking bust, as she always did, and passed down the corridor to the canteen. She could tell that something unusual was happening when she walked in. The normal people were there—doctors, nurses, porters, clerical and ancillary staff—but there seemed to be an air of suppressed excitement. She wondered why.

Dan was sitting at their favorite table in the corner. He was obviously looking out for her and waved at her exuberantly. Facing him, and with his back to her, was a man in a brown suit. She walked over and Dan stood to greet her. His smile was even wider than usual.

'I've got a surprise, Sue. I've got our top-of-the-bill act. Someone I know you'll have heard of. Geordie Summers.' He turned to the other man at the table. 'Geordie, this is Sue McCain, a very good friend of mine.'

Her face froze. This was a living nightmare. It couldn't be happening to her! Not five seconds ago she'd been so happy, and now... How did he...? Why Geordie of all people?

Geordie stood and turned. When he saw her he, too, looked incredulous. 'Why it's—' he started.

She had to act. She lunged forward, hugged him and kissed him. 'Geordie, it's so good to see you again. What a surprise!' Turning to Dan, she said, 'Geordie and I are old friends. In fact, he was the only acquaintance of my late husband that I didn't hate.'

She could tell from their expressions that both Dan and Geordie were a bit dubious about that. Smiling desperately at Dan, she said, 'Look, I'm parched. Could you get me a cup of tea? And perhaps a sandwich? I rushed out when you phoned.'

'Of course,' he said, and walked to the serving counter. But he was frowning.

She sat opposite Geordie. In almost any other circumstances she would have been delighted to see him again. 'Still a health fanatic, I see,' she teased gently, looking at the salad and glass of milk in front of him.

'Still a health fanatic,' he agreed. 'No drink, no drugs, not even tea or coffee. I haven't changed at all. But what happened to you? We missed you. You've changed.'

Geordie was a pop singer, perhaps slightly older than most. He had first made it big about ten years ago, and had had three or four hits. But he'd been wise enough to know that he couldn't stay at the top, and so had turned himself into more of a cabaret performer. He'd had a couple of series on TV, worked up and down the country on tour, presented a radio show. His audience now was much larger than the teenagers he had first sung for.

She didn't have much time. 'Listen,' she said, 'you knew me through my ex-husband. He was a record producer, we met at parties and so on. That's all, nothing else.'

Geordie looked as if he couldn't believe this. 'But you were—'

'My name's Sue McCain. I'm a recently qualified midwife. I started a new life here. Please, don't spoil it, Geordie'

'Is Dan Webster part of the new life?'

'I hope he will be,' she said miserably.

'I just don't understand this.' Geordie looked baffled. 'First you—'

'You don't have to understand it. If you want, we'll talk about it later. But for now just cover up for me.'

'All right. I will. But I'm not very happy about it. I've only just met him, but I like Dan Webster.'

'So do I,' she told him.

Dan arrived back at their table, carrying a tray. She glanced up at him fearfully, and saw he looked thoughtful. Then she steeled herself. She had done nothing wrong!

'I don't think I told you,' she said. 'My ex-husband hung around on the fringes of show business. He was supposed to be a record producer. And that's where I met Geordie. We got to talk a lot at parties because we were the only two people who didn't drink.'

'I didn't like Doug Jones,' Geordie said. 'Not only was he a creep, he was a lousy record producer. You're well rid of him.'

'Only Dan knows I was once married,' Sue said, 'so don't broadcast it. OK?'

Troubled, Geordie glanced from Dan to her. 'I can understand you wanting to keep it quiet. I'll say nothing.'

She reached for the tea Dan had brought her.

'Change of unpleasant subject,' she said. 'How come you volunteered for this job, Geordie?'

Her friend laughed and pointed to Dan. 'Ask this man,' he said. 'And "volunteered" is not the right word.'

'One of the porters who has been here for years told me that a singer had been born here a long time ago,' Dan said. 'So I looked through the records, worked out it was Geordie here and phoned him.'

'Actually, I volunteered like a shot,' Geordie said. 'My ma always said how well she was treated here, so it was the least I could do. and the band was very happy, too. We do a bit of charity work here and there.'

Dan was enthusiastic. 'You'll be a great top of the bill and you'll fill the theatre. I'm going to ask if we can run an extra night. We'll make a fortune!'

She smiled at his excitement. 'It should be a good show,' she agreed. 'Geordie, I'll see you about a bit. I'm the assistant stage manager—I help a man called Max Morgan.'

'I'll bet you're a good manager,' he said. 'Now, tell me about this job as midwife…'

That night both Megan and Jane were away. Jane was on nights, and Megan had gone for a short holiday—she needed one after her troubles. Dan was at the theatre with Geordie and Max, talking about the format of the show. Sue had to attend an evening lecture on new developments in pain relief techniques for midwives, so she couldn't be with them. But she phoned the theatre when she got home and asked to speak to Dan.

'I thought I'd go to bed early,' she said. 'If I leave

a key under the big plant pot in the drive, would you like to come round and let yourself in?'

Dan was troubled. 'I don't think Mickey would think much of that as an idea,' he said first of all, 'but I suppose you could leave it there just this once.'

'I won't do it again. But I want you to come round, Dan, I really do.'

'And I want to come. I'm not sure when we'll finish here, though. Max and Geordie have done nothing but disagree since they met.'

'That's a good sign,' Sue said. 'It means they're concerned about the show. It'll all come right in the end.' Then she added quickly, 'Or so I would have thought.'

'I'm sure you're right.' Once again she could detect the doubt in Dan's voice. But there was nothing she could do about it. For a start, neither of them liked displays of emotion over the phone.

There was the sound of distant shouting over the phone, and he said quickly, 'I'm needed again. See you later, sweetheart.' And he was gone. She sighed as she replaced the receiver.

She wanted to make things all right. First she made him a small supper tray and placed it by the bed as she knew he'd be hungry. She showered, dabbed herself with scent and put on a pretty white silk nightie. Then she got into bed and tried to read the notes from the lecture she had heard. They didn't make much sense to her.

It was exciting, hearing the key in the lock, the sound of footsteps on the stairs. Then he was in her bedroom, and she reached out her arms to greet him.

'You smell wonderful,' he said after the first long kiss, 'and you feel wonderful, too.'

'You smell a bit sweaty,' she replied, 'but I think I like it. What have you been doing?'

'Heaving stuff around the stage for Max and Geordie. I like working for them and I need the exercise. You were right, by the way. The two of them are the best of friends now.' He stood and pulled the rough sweater over his head. 'Could I have a bath or a shower? I'm not getting into bed, smelling like this, with a fragrant girl like you.'

'Have a shower. Then you'll be in bed with me quicker. And I've done you a supper tray.'

He kissed her again. 'You're marvellous. How did you know I'd be ravenous?'

He was back in five minutes, damp and exciting. The towel round his waist dropped and he scrambled into bed and reached for her. 'Have your supper first,' she scolded. 'I went to a lot of trouble to make it for you.'

'First?' he asked. 'What's second, then?'

She blushed, then rallied. 'You looked tired. I want you to have a good night's sleep.'

So he ate the sandwiches while she made him tea with a kettle she had brought to the bedroom. 'That was good,' he sighed when he had finished. 'You're good to me, Sue.' He kissed her. 'Now. We have to talk.'

She frowned . 'Why talk? Can't we just…do things? You must be tired.'

He shook his head. Sadly, he said, 'We have to talk, Sue. I've been with Geordie all evening. All the time he was evasive about you. It's good of him to help us and obviously I didn't push him, but he thinks a lot of you and he's uncomfortable about the situation.'

'Yes,' said Sue miserably. She should have known that she couldn't fool Dan for long.

Dan went on, 'I know…well, I think I know that there's nothing between you two. I know there's a lot of your previous life that you haven't told me about. Now I'm going to say something that you've always stopped me saying in the past. I love you, Sue. And I think you love me. Don't you?'

He had asked her. She had to reply. 'Yes,' she said, after a pause.

'You know all about me, every last detail you could want to know. But I don't know all about you. There has to be trust between us, it's all-important. Can't you tell me? I know there's something.'

'I've never done anything wrong,' she said. 'And I can tell you I've never been anything but a friend to Geordie. But I can't tell you the rest—I just can't.'

The silence between them stretched interminably. Then he leaned over to kiss her, and said, with a quiet reserve that was new, 'I think I'd better go. I'll dress in the bathroom. I'll lock the door and push the keys through the letter-box.'

He walked out of her bedroom. She knew she could call him back, and he would have returned like a shot. She desperately wanted to call him back, but something prevented her. There was the sound of footsteps on the stair, the front door closed and then there was the tinkle of the key. She lay down and wept.

CHAPTER EIGHT

SUE was tired but there was no way she could sleep. At three in the morning she sat up and reached for her mobile phone. She would call Dan. But something stopped her. You didn't ring a busy doctor at this time unless it was really important. Only when it was nearly dawn did she manage to get a couple of hours' rest.

Finally she was awakened by the ringing of the doorbell. It was ten o'clock. She went downstairs to find a delivery man with a massive bunch of red and yellow roses. Inside the bunch was a card. 'Sorry for pushing too soon' it said. It made her feel worse.

Once again she reached for her phone. She would arrange a meeting and tell him everything. But some dead weight held her back. She couldn't tell him, not yet. She wanted just to be a midwife. And she knew that once she had revealed all, no matter how much he loved her he would never quite think of her in the same way again. It wouldn't be possible. Or would it?

She couldn't stay in and she didn't want to go to the hospital, so she would have to visit someone. There must be a friend somewhere she could just be with. She didn't want to talk. Rain hammered on the roof of her car as she dived inside. She would visit William.

By now she was known by the staff, and was waved through straight to the place where William did most of his work. She went through the outer greenhouse and gave a shout to let him know she was there. He

147

appeared at the door, obviously pleased to see her. 'Come in, come in. Gemma is here again.'

Gemma was dressed in overalls and she had on a pair of rubber gloves. In her hand was a trowel. 'I'll soon be as expert at bringing plants into the world as I am at bringing babies into it,' she said.

Sue had to smile at the obvious happiness of her friend. 'You've been here a while?'

Gemma turned slightly pink. 'I've got a few days off. William asked me if I'd like to stay with him for a while. See what his kind of work was like. It's very restful after being a midwife.'

'Come and see how my propagating is coming along,' William called. 'My latest plant is doing really well. Strong, and some good colour developing now. I think it's a winner.'

She walked over to look at the plant. 'I'm going to call it after you, if you don't mind,' William said. 'Lovely lady, lovely flower.'

'But, William, what about…? Sue said uncertainly.

'I'm going to start from scratch with Gemma,' William said. 'Grow her a completely new plant. But I had in mind naming this after you since the moment you called. It'll be a bright silver.'

'Silver,' said Sue, a catch in her throat. 'Silver.' He didn't know.

Afterwards she went to the hospital. There was no way she was going to nurse her hurt like a prima donna. Dan had sent her flowers so the least she could do was go to see him.

Eventually she found him in the canteen. He was on his own, at the table they had shared so often. It was only twenty-four hours since she'd seen him there last, and such a lot had happened! She braced herself, and went across to him, hoping that he would welcome her. He had sent her flowers.

He looked up as she stood in front of his table. 'Sue! I'm so glad to see you!'

She could tell by his eyes that he meant it, and she felt that a great weight had been lifted from her. She sat opposite him. 'I'm so glad to see you, too,' she said. 'You don't know how much.' She paused a minute and then went on, 'Look, the canteen at lunchtime is no place for baring my soul. I just want you to know that you are very important to me, no one more so. It's just that...I need time. Surely you can let me have that?'

He sighed. 'Yes,' he said, 'you can have anything you want from me. I'll say it again. I love you, Sue.'

She said nothing, but reached over and squeezed his hand. 'Not long,' she said. 'It won't be long, it can't be.'

After a while she continued, 'Thank you for the flowers. I really think I should have sent them to you. But...but I really appreciated them. And you've nothing to be sorry for. I have.'

'Sue!' he said, and his voice had changed. It was the Dan she knew, the man who reassured everybody in the middle of a gynaecological emergency, the man who always kept calm when things were going wrong. 'I don't like it when you're penitent. I prefer you when you're awkward and looking for a fight. We've got a show to put on and we've got to support each other. We can weep and wail after that.'

'Whatever happens, I'm not going to weep and wail. Now, I'm going to help Max this afternoon as I've got the time off. Any chance of you dropping in?'

'None. Babies come just as normal. I'm a working man again.' He checked his watch. 'In fact, I'm a working man in five minutes.'

'I'll be in touch. Bye, Dan.' She walked away. As she did she thought over what he had just done. He had deliberately quietened the situation down, given her the time she'd asked for and tried to ensure that she didn't worry. He was a good man, she thought.

'And this is Sue McCain, my assistant stage manager,' Max said. 'Considering she knows nothing about what she's doing, she's managing very well.'

'I'll bet she is,' said Geordie. 'Hi, Sue.'

She was glad Geordie hadn't mentioned that they had met before. She didn't feel like going into explanations and half-lies. And Max wouldn't be as gentle as Dan had been.

The three of them worked through Geordie's act, Sue taking notes of what would be required and when. Geordie's band and his two roadies would be coming in later. They had been together for years.

'They're all good lads,' Geordie said. 'They don't break up hotels and so on. Well, not any more.' It was only a small backing group—a drummer, two guitar players and a keyboard player—but they were all expert musicians. 'They'll be coming in the van in an hour or so,' Geordie said.

Sue remembered the van—it was vast. 'Where are you going to park the van?' she asked. 'We can't leave it on the street outside for long.'

It was Max who came up with an answer. 'There's Mullard's store next door,' he said. 'They might let us leave it in their delivery yard. That would be really handy. Sue, get Geordie a coffee or something and I'll just nip round and ask them.'

Sue and Geordie faced each other in the middle of the empty stage. 'I'm not happy,' Geordie said. 'I don't want a coffee. I want a talk. Where can we go?'

She took him into a dressing room and fetched two coffees anyway. She didn't really want one, but it would give her something to do with her hands. Then she sat facing him and tried to relax.

'I know how your husband treated you, and perhaps I can guess how you felt about the death of your baby,' Geordie said. 'I even know that you weren't always too keen on what you did. But you were good.'

'I just had to get away,' she muttered. 'I wanted my life back.'

'You had some good friends,' he went on remorselessly. 'I like to think I was one. Good friends who cared for you. You cut them all off. One minute you were in hospital, then you disappeared. We tried like mad to get some idea from that solicitor of yours, but he was like an iron door. He even said he would deal with any letters.'

'I told him to burn everything personal,' she said, 'but I'm sorry now. Then I was just so…sorry for myself. Only afterwards did I realise I'd cut myself off from something—some people that I would miss.'

'Like the rest of my group? They're all looking forward to seeing you again.'

'The group! Geordie, will you ask them to—?'

'I already have done. In fact, I've told them, not asked them. After all, I'm the boss. They'll keep your secret.' He grinned and the mood changed. 'So you just cleared out and left the job behind. I must say there are times I've thought of doing the same myself. Are you happy in your new job?'

'I love it. It's all I ever wanted.'

'And this fellow, Dan Webster. What d'you feel about him?'

'You haven't told him anything?' she said in panic.

'No. But he's shrewd, you can't keep much from him. Two things, Sue. One, he'll be good for you. I know that. Two, you're not doing him right by not telling him. Trust him.'

'I want to, I want to,' she said. 'But over the past four and a half years I've hidden it and now I—'

'Here you both are,' Max said, bursting through the door, a thick roll of papers under his arm. 'No problems with next door—they're very happy for you to park the van there, Geordie. Just one thing. If you could see your way to dropping in on them and giving them a couple of signed photographs and so on? They might get round to sponsoring us then.'

'Happy to,' said Geordie obligingly. 'If you're doing the job, do it well. We'll make money for this hospital somehow. What's that under your arm, Max?'

'Ah! I brought them in to show you. You've got to hand it to Dan Webster, he's a fast mover. What d'you think of your posters?' Max unrolled a poster from the roll under his arm and displayed it.

'That's pretty good,' Geordie said.

Max sighed. 'Dan should run the country. He phoned the best poster firm in the north of England, asked for these to be designed, printed and then put up. Fast, please. And would you do it for nothing?'

'He does tend to get his way,' Geordie said. 'Now, the lighting plan for my second number, Max. The song is slow and rather sad so I want a dimmer here and here...'

It was just one of those things, and perhaps in some ways it was preferable. Hospital life was like that. The consultant was away for a fortnight, a couple of mid-wives were off ill, there seemed to be an excess of babies being born, and too many of those were diffi-cult. The department was run off its feet.

She knew that Dan was working like a lunatic. Nothing, of course, would be allowed to get in the way of his professional duties. And he managed them with such calmness, such apparent ease!

But the work with the concert was taking vast amounts of his time. There were people to phone, sponsorships to be discussed, special guests to be in-vited. Sue saw a side of him that she had only sus-pected. Dan was a magnificent organizer. Perhaps only she knew how much time he put in. And all the time he remained amiable and serene.

Through the next ten days she saw little of him. She phoned him at least once each day, and they had oc-casional meetings on the ward or in the delivery suite. She thought of him constantly, but her thoughts never seemed to get anywhere.

He seemed to have returned to his old imperturbable self. He was happy, smiling cheerful. Then one day he whispered to her in the corridor, 'Just because I don't say anything, it doesn't mean that I don't think or feel.' And then she knew that he was suffering, too.

They would wait till after the concert. Then she...What would she do then? Whenever she tried to think, the past rose up like a concrete wall and there was no way she could climb it or knock it down. The fact that she had built the wall herself didn't help at all.

The concert was to run for four evenings, from Wednesday to Saturday. She had arranged her shifts so she could be off the entire week. Max would need help in the few days before the show.

She wasn't sure if she was looking forward to the work. One half of her was, the other half could foresee problems. But somehow she would survive. Then, on the Monday before the Wednesday of the first performance, her world was knocked apart again.

It was quite early in the morning and she was at home, expecting to go round to the theatre in the afternoon. Her phone rang—it was Max. His voice sounded harsh and strained. 'Come now to St. Leonard's Hospital,' he rasped. 'Ward Thirteen. We're waiting for you. This is an emergency.'

'Ward Thirteen—what's that?' she asked stupidly.

'Apparently, it's Orthopaedics. Now stop asking questions and get here. I told you, this is an emergency!' He rang off.

What was happening? Max did tend to exaggerate things—it was part of his character—but she thought she'd detected genuine panic in his voice. Something bad had happened.

St. Leonard's Hospital was at the other side of town, but she still got there quickly. She rode up to Ward Thirteen and was somehow recognized at once by a rather excited ward clerk. 'You'll be for Mr Summers,' she said. 'He's in a side ward down there. I'll take you.'

'Geordie Summers? But what's he doing in…?'

She was showed into a small side room. There were two visitors, Max and Dan, both looking extremely worried. On the bed, looking white-faced through pain, and with a great mound where his right leg should be, lay Geordie Summers. 'I've broken my leg,' said Geordie. 'I've broken it really badly.'

'A compound fracture of the tibia and fibula,' Dan said, referring to the two bones of the lower leg. 'Geordie's going to require some quite expert surgery.'

'It might be serious,' said Max, who apparently couldn't care less. 'The most important thing is there's no way he'll be on stage in three days.'

'Geordie insisted I send for you,' said Dan. Sue could tell that he didn't know why, and he was rather upset. 'I've got things to do,' he went on. 'I'll have to organize a set of new posters, saying that the head of the bill is incapable of performing. I never thought to insure against this, though I will next time. But we can't take people's money and not have the main act.'

Geordie was obviously in pain 'Right,' he said to Max and Dan, 'you two, out. Use your influence with the ward clerk and try to get some coffee. And don't make any decisions till you come back in here. I'm going to talk to Sue for a minute.'

Max was too gloomy to notice he'd been dismissed. But Sue saw Dan glance from her to Geordie, obviously wondering what was happening. She didn't know herself, but she had an uneasy idea. 'Come back in ten minutes,' she said. The two men left.

'What happened?' she asked, knowing however, that small talk wasn't what Geordie wanted.

'Some sweet but daft old lady ran me down in the park,' he said. 'I'd gone for my early morning run, and she tried to slow to let me pass. A car with automatic transmission. Her foot slipped from the brake to the accelerator. She hit me—wham!'

'Ow!' said Sue.

'Quite so. I got the full treatment then—police, ambulance, even the local press. Us old troupers make the most of every photo opportunity. But that's not why you're here. You know what I'm going to say.'

'At a guess, the show must go on,' she said bitterly.

'Yes, the show must go one! Either it's cancelled or—'

'I can't, Geordie, I haven't for four and a half years. I'm a midwife now. It's all I want to be.'

'You can be a midwife! But just for four nights be something else.' Still she hesitated, and he went on angrily, 'For goodness' sake, Sue, that man loves you. He'd do anything for you! So do something for him!'

He was driving her into a corner. 'But…I'm scared,' she said.

'Everyone is scared when they first get on stage. I'm always scared. The thing you do is get on there and get over it.'

There was a pause. 'You'll never forgive yourself if you don't,' he said gently.

'I'm also a bit scared that I might…like it too much.'

'You never did like it as much as the rest of us did. You're a midwife now and that's what you'll stay.'

She took a deep breath, straightened her shoulders and wished her smile were a little less strained. Then she went to the door and waved to the two outside. They had charmed the ward clerk and got their coffee.

'Come up with any world-shaking ideas?' Max asked as he closed the door.

'Yes,' said Geordie. 'You're going to love this.'

'We've got a replacement for him,' Sue said faltering ly.

'Even bigger than me,' Geordie said, his smile hiding the pain he was now feeling. 'And, what's more, this is a come-back. It'll make the national news.'

Sue saw Dan's eyes flickering between her and Geordie. He was obviously perplexed, wondering what was happening. She wanted desperately for him to understand, so she spoke straight to him. 'I didn't used to be known as Sue,' she said. 'I had another name. I was called Silver McCain.'

Dan had no real idea of female pop stars, but even he had heard that name. 'Wasn't she a singer?' he asked, puzzled.

Max had more idea. He looked at her disbelievingly. 'You were England's biggest pop star—oh, five years ago,' he said. You were having a baby and the baby died. Then you just disappeared. The papers were full of you. You were magnificent.'

'I became a midwife,' Sue said.

'Well, I've tried to make sure the show goes on,' Geordie said, and the others realised from his voice just how much pain he was in. 'And I'm sorry I broke my leg, but I've done what I can. Now, if you don't mind, I could do with a rest. You lot have arrangements to make. Sue, you can do it!'

'I'll do it,' she said.

'Good. Now give me a kiss, and get to work. My lads will be pleased to work with you again. You'd better see them this morning—you've got a lot of rehearsing to do.'

'We'll be in touch, 'Dan said, and they left.

In the lift going down she looked at Dan and tried to guess what he was feeling. He seemed remote, as if not quite understanding what was happening. She had to get through to him, 'I tried to tell you, Dan,' she said. 'I would have in time. It was just that…somehow I couldn't.'

'I would have understood,' he said. 'It was nothing to be ashamed of. Just the opposite, I would have said. I wish you'd chosen to confide in me.'

'Just a minute,' Max said sharply. 'You two may have personal problems, but at the moment they don't matter. You can sort them out after the show. Until Saturday night the show is all-important. After that time you can get married, engaged, divorced, I just don't care. But until then there are no personality clashes at all. Understood?'

Dan and Sue glanced at each other. Then both nodded.

'Good. Now, Dan, this is really big. Get in touch with that poster agency—we want banners over the posters—''The return of Silver McCain!'' Sue I'm going to ring up a press agent and set up a conference tomorrow morning. There'll be a photo call and a press conference and you're to have a story ready— OK?'

'OK,' she said dully. This was old stuff.

'Then remember to smile! You've agreed to do the job—do it right. Dan, I've got a contact number. We might be able to sell the programme to a TV company. That OK, Sue?'

'Good idea,' she said.

Max's mind was still running excitedly over all the possibilities. 'Have you still got an agent, Sue? Dan, perhaps we ought to have a formal contract with Sue. She's a big name and—'

'No,' said Dan. 'I'm not having a formal contract. This is a question of trust.'

Sue wondered if he knew just how much using that word had hurt her. But she merely said, 'There's no need for a contract and I don't have an agent. When I left singing I got a good lawyer to cut me off from all responsibilities. I can do what I like now.'

Dan's mobile phone rang. 'Yes, Freddy? How long has that been? No, you did right? I'm on my way and I should be about twenty minutes.'

He turned to them and said, for once, she thought, seeming weary, 'I've got to go. The medical job takes priority.'

'I'll come over to the hospital later,' Sue said, 'and perhaps we can—'

'Not till a long time later,' interrupted Max. 'You've forgotten a lot, sweetheart. This job comes first!'

They were now in the hospital car park. Each had a separate car. She told Max she'd see him at the theatre at once, then hurried after Dan.

'Dan! I wish I'd been able to tell you in my own time. I would have told you. You might not think it much, but it is—it was—to me.'

He turned, and there was a touch of the old smile. 'I love you,' he said, 'but now I have work to do. And so do you.'

'Silver! Sweetheart, what happened to you? It's so good to see you...' She stood in the middle of the stage and tried to kiss four men at once.

She hadn't been looking forward to meeting Geordie's band again. They were old friends, and she had had to ask that they pretend they didn't know her.

She knew this would have hurt them—as it had hurt Geordie. But now it was all right.

Geordie had phoned them from hospital, had told them that he had broken his leg and that plans had been changed. Silver McCain would sing again, and they would back her.

Griff, Peter, Malcolm and Stevie. It was good to be with them again. They had toured together, with her at the top of the bill. She had got on better with them than she had with her own backing group, who had usually been session musicians hired by her husband.

'What're you going to sing, Silver?' Griff, the drummer, asked. 'We know most of your stuff so it won't take us long to get in behind you. And you never had really fancy arrangements. Just that great voice.'

'We'll talk about that now,' Max said, walking on stage. 'We're going to have to rewrite the whole of the second half. In two and a half days!'

'No problem,' said Sue. 'I can do it.' There was a sick feeling in the pit of her stomach, half apprehension, half excitement. She had forgotten it. But it was coming back.

There were two halves to the programme. In the first half was the choir and other acts Dan had managed to find. The second half had been given entirely to Geordie. Now she would have to fill it.

She sat with Max and the others and worked out her programme. 'You never used to say anything between songs,' said Stevie, the bass guitarist. 'That...your husband used to introduce the songs. D'you want one of us to do it? Or Max?'

'I'll do my own continuity stuff,' she said. 'If I'm just singing and talking to friends, I can do it.'

There was the lighting plan to work out, the layout on stage, the order of the songs. At home she still had the sheets of her songs, but her performances had always been voice-led. All the band had to do was provide backing. She told them she'd bring the sheets in the next day.

'Right,' said Max after a while. 'I think that's enough talking for one morning. Now, the band says they can handle backing to the first song, the one you first did well with. "You left me", it's called? So let's get through it. Jut start like you used to.'

Suddenly it was all too real. This was what they had been talking about, but now it was real. She felt sick and dizzy and wished she were at home, at work, anywhere but here. But she wasn't. She had to do it. For Dan if for no other reason.

The roadies had set up the band's instruments and all the other complex electronic gadgetry. She walked to the front of the stage, listening to the once familiar sounds of the group at practice—drumbeats, riffs on the guitars, arpeggios from the keyboard.

She stood at the microphone. She seemed to be alone on stage. In front of her were rows of empty seats, galleries, boxes, and in three days they'd all be filled. So often she had seen it before, and always it had terrified her. She had got over it—then.

She heard the soft, eight-bar introduction. She should have come in on the next note, but she didn't—or couldn't.

'Don't worry,' Max called. 'Take your time. The band will go through it again.'

It wasn't a hard song. It started on one low note, and repeated the same note for six bars. This time she tried to come in. She managed to sing but she knew she was slightly off key as she started. But she improved.

'I thought I had you but then you were gone. I thought I had love but then there was none. I thought that your promise was honest and true. I knew I had pain but I thought I had you.' Then there were three loud beats of the drum. *'And you left me!'* Her voice soared an octave, doubled in volume.

And it all came back. She was on stage, she could do it. The rest of the song was easy. She felt at home now.

The band had guessed what she was feeling and clapped as she finished. She turned and gave them a little curtsey.

'That first line again,' said Max. 'I know you can do it, but I want to hear it.'

He worked them through till late afternoon. By the end of that time she had her confidence back. She could sing. She enjoyed it.

'Pretty good that, Silver,' Griff said. 'No one could tell that you'd had a four-year layoff.'

'Tell you what,' said Stevie, 'you're better than you were. You've got more…bottom than you had.'

She thrilled a little at this. These were experts. They knew what they were talking about—they didn't give praise easily.

'Are you going to come back with us, Silver?' asked Griff. 'Tour and sing with Geordie? It would be just like old times.'

That had been the wrong thing to say. 'No,' she said.

CHAPTER NINE

Now there were more problems to tackle—starting with Jane and Megan. Fortunately both of them were in when she arrived home. Painful past experience told Sue that if she stayed at her house there would be a constant procession of unwanted visitors—the press, fans and those merely curious, wanting to see a 'real singer'. She would move into the hotel with Geordie's band. The hotel was used to celebrity guests, and would protect her.

'I hope you don't feel I'm being unfriendly,' she said, 'but I'm going to move into a hotel for a bit. And I've got things to tell you.'

Her two friends were incredulous, then amazed, then impressed. 'I've been living with a star, and I didn't know it,' squeaked Jane. 'I've got nieces and nephews who'll want your autograph. I've even got some of your CDs.'

'I know,' said Sue. 'Did you never notice I went into the kitchen when you played them?'

She felt a slight touch of panic. Already these two, her tried and trusted friends, were treating her as if she were someone different. She wanted to stay one of them!

'Look,' she said, 'I didn't want this. It will be over by Saturday night. On Monday I start back on the delivery suite on nights. I'm Sue McCain, a midwife.'

'Are you sure?' asked Jane. 'Will you still want to be a midwife after you've been on stage for four nights, singing and listening to the applause? Will they let you become a midwife again?'

'I don't want to be a singer again,' Sue cried desperately. 'I don't think I ever did. I want to deliver babies, be a simple midwife. I want to hang around here with you two and gossip. I've had the other life and I hated it.'

She didn't realise how upset she sounded. Jane stood and put her arm around her comfortingly. 'You're carrying a lot, love,' she said. 'But you can do it and we'll help. And, by the sound of things, you'll make a fortune for the hospital.'

It was good to be with friends. 'How's Dan taking the news?' asked Megan. 'He did know, didn't he?'

'No,' sighed Sue. 'I never got round to telling him. I didn't want to. I wanted to forget it all myself. With any luck he'll be all right. But I think he's finding it a bit of a…shock.'

'He's a good man,' said Megan judiciously. 'He might find it difficult, but he'll cope. He's got…balance.'

Sue found things a bit better then.

After answering all sorts of eager questions, she went up to her bedroom. Behind her she could hear the dull thump of one of her CDs. Jane had dug it out and asked if Sue minded if they played it. 'Not at all,' Sue had said. 'I'll have to get used to it. I guess I'm going to hear the music quite a bit over the next few days.'

Sue's first task was to pack two large suitcases. She needed to keep away from home completely, knowing that if there was no sighting of her at all people would soon tire of coming round. For a while it might be hard on her two friends, dealing with oddball callers,

but they didn't seem to mind. 'I'm quite looking forward to being known as the intimate friend of a star,'
Jane had said with a giggle.

When the suitcases were packed she paused, then
gritted her teeth. It had to be done. Hers was the biggest bedroom, and in the corner was a tiny boxroom.
She kept junk in there, kept it locked and seldom went
inside. From the back of a drawer she took out the
key.

The first box she opened held her sheet music.
Quickly she riffled through it to check that everything
she needed was there. She'd take it all to Geordie's
lads tomorrow—they'd have no trouble reading it.
Probably they could manage quite well without it.

The second case hadn't been opened in four years.
A riot of emotions coursed through her as she forced
up the lid and lifted aside sheets of tissue paper. There
was no musty smell, just the faint scent of the fresh
lavender she had used. Now she remembered how
carefully she had packed. It had been as if she'd been
laying down a part of her life for ever. And now she
was taking up that life again!

She lifted out the outfits and laid them carefully on
the bed. A trouser suit, a mini-dress, a long dress slit
up to the thigh. And all in silver sequins, her trade
mark. She was Silver McCain. There was a long box
there and she opened that, shaking out the long silver
wig.

She might as well do the job properly. She sat at
the dressing-table and took out the make-up that had
been unused for so long—the darker eye shadow and
mascara, the brighter lipstick. Then she took a packet
of sparkling tights from the trunk, pulled on a pair,
wriggled into the mini-dress, adjusted the wig and

walked downstairs. Her two friends were still sitting in the kitchen.

'Recognise me?' she asked.

There was silence for a moment.

'Oh, Sue, where have you gone?' asked Megan.

Later, Megan and Jane went out. Sue took off her outfit and put on a tracksuit, then phoned the hospital. Dan was in Theatre so she left a message, asking him to phone her when he was free, no matter how late it might be. She felt lost.

In desperation she made herself a mug of coffee, huddled into a thick coat and walked down to the arbour. It was cold and dark, of course, but the familiar surroundings settled her. But now no longer could it be the refuge she had built. She was deliberately going back into the world she had built the refuge to escape from. Taking out her mobile phone, she gazed at the green screen, willing the phone to ring. It didn't.

In fact, it didn't ring until quite late that night when she was sitting on the bed, after having a bath to try and relax. She grabbed it before it had chance to ring again. It was Dan, but he sounded tired and cautious.

'How are you?' she asked. 'How did the operation go?'

She guessed the answer in the pause before he replied. 'Not too well,' he said, the pain in his voice obvious. 'The baby died. But it never had much of a chance. It was far too early and I suppose we expected it.'

'I know how it hurts,' she said, 'but, other than that, are you all right?'

'A bit confused,' he admitted. 'Today has been

busy. There have been too many shocks, too much work.'

'Sometimes it's like that in hospital,' she said, 'and you've had...other surprises as well.' She said it cautiously, and was infinitely relieved when she heard him laugh.

'You could say that,' he said. 'Look, Sue, I've had a chance to think about what you're doing, what you're letting yourself in for, what you're giving. It's an awful lot. I love you for it, and I love you anyway. Now, tell me what stage we're up to with the show.'

After that it was easier. Their discussion was then purely to do with the show and the arrangements she had made, and as ever he swiftly got absorbed in it. 'I'm going to bed,' he said finally. 'I need to. Phone me any time, Sue—and if you don't I understand.'

She felt better then, and she managed to sleep.

In the morning she drove round to the theatre and left her stage gear there, then went to the hotel and deposited her two large trunks. She had booked a suite on the same floor as Geordie's band. Once settled in the suite, she phoned Geordie's ward. The sister told her that his operation had been a complete success. Then she was put through to him.

After asking how things were going, he said, 'I'm glad you're doing this, Sue. It'll lay some ghosts for you, and it'll bring a fair amount of money into the hospital. Think that you're doing it for my ma. She would have liked to have had you as a midwife.'

'No way would I have wanted to have been responsible for bringing you into the world, Geordie Summers,' she said. 'I've got enough on my conscience already.'

He laughed. 'You know what we always say in show business—break a leg! Well, I'm never going to say it to anyone again. Ow! And I'm giving up laughing for ever.'

She rang off. Now she was realising that her years as a singer hadn't been all bad. She had made some good friends.

Her next stop was to talk to the band, enjoying a late and leisurely breakfast in the sitting room they all shared. She gave out the sheet music and talked through what they were to play. There would be no difficulty. These were professionals—besides, they had backed her before on occasion. Everything would be all right. Feeling slightly more confident, she drove down to the theatre. This morning was scheduled for a complete dress rehearsal for the first half of the programme. She might be singing in the second half herself, but she knew Max would still need her as a gopher.

It came as a bit of a surprise to find that Max had got a substitute for her—her friend Stella Robinson. Dan had sent down an extra midwife.

Being his usual brusque self, Max said, 'I know you want to do the job, Sue, but you can't. You've got enough to do and you'll only mess up if you do too much. So this morning you show Stella here what to do, and from then on she does it. OK?'

Sue thought for a moment. It did make sense. 'Of course it's OK,' she said. 'But I'm available for help if I'm needed.'

Max went to organise the first of the acts. Stella turned to her, agog. 'It's true, isn't it? You're Silver McCain? The whole hospital is talking about you.

Why didn't you tell anybody? We'd have loved to know.'

'I just wanted a quiet life,' Sue said sadly. 'Now, working for Max isn't easy—he likes things done exactly right. These lists are...'

She was happy in the handover. Stella had a midwife's training and knew exactly how to prioritise, what to write down, how to calm people who got into a flap. She knew not to panic. Sue knew she'd be good at the job.

The morning dress rehearsal went well. The choir and the acts were good, and fitted well on stage. Max had been working with each act individually, now it was good to see them working as a whole. One or two people wanted to talk to the newly discovered Silver McCain, but Max wouldn't let them. 'She's working,' he shouted. 'Leave her alone.' When the rehearsal was over, and they finally broke for lunch, she knew Max was pleased—though he wouldn't say so.

She noticed that quite a lot of people who had rehearsed were sitting in the theatre, or were coming back, bringing sandwiches and drinks with them. She was puzzled. 'Why aren't they all leaving?' she asked Max.

'They're staying to see you,' Max said. 'They won't have a chance otherwise.'

Sue frowned. Then she waved back at Jane, who was sitting with a group of friends. 'I suppose that's all right,' she said.

Stella came towards them, clutching her mobile phone. 'It's Dan Webster for you,' she said to Max.

Max took the phone. 'I see... Guess so... It's a good idea. I'll ask her.' Turning to Sue, he said abruptly. 'D'you mind if Dan sends some hospital people down this afternoon to watch you? They'll be working nights the rest of the week.'

'All right,' she said after a pause, 'but why didn't he ask me?'

'He didn't because he asked me, and I'm the stage manager,' snapped Max. 'But you can talk to him now.' He thrust the phone at her and walked away, taking Stella with him.

'Dan?' she asked.

It was good to hear his voice. 'You're scared,' he said, 'wondering if you've done the right thing. Well, you have done the right thing, so get out there and enjoy it.'

'How d'you know what I'm thinking?' she asked. 'You've got it exactly right.'

'I know because I think a lot about you. Now, get to it. I love you.'

It's surprising how easy it is to say it now, she thought. Why hadn't she done so before? 'I love you, too,' she said.

Max had closed the curtains and she peered from the wings. The front of the theatre was filling. There was a definite buzz of excitement. She could see people she knew, people she had trained with, worked with. She saw Freddy Sharp there, secretly holding the hand of a trainee midwife. Sue grinned. That gave her a touch of perspective. Some things were the same. It seemed that all of the hospital staff who could get away had come.

Max came up to her. 'You'd better get ready now. It's a dress rehearsal, so full kit.'

The band and the roadies were setting up the instruments on stage. There was the normal rattle of drums, chords from the guitars. The sounds seemed to excite the audience.

A full dress rehearsal. She went to her dressing room. How it brought back memories! The towel in front of her, the make-up bag not used for so long. Stage make-up wasn't like normal makeup. She sat there in her underwear and felt a sudden burst of horror. She couldn't do this, didn't want to do this! She was a midwife. Her heart was beating far too fast, her breath rate growing faster. She was panicking.

There were emergencies in midwifery, too, and she had learned how to cope. She closed her eyes, relaxed every muscle she could, willed her breathing to slow. Her heart settled to its normal pace. She could do it.

She was to wear two outfits—the trouser suit first and then the long dress. She called for Stella, gave her the gown and told her what to do. Then Stella watched, amazed as Sue slipped into the trouser suit, and then pulled on the long wig.

'Sue, you're so different!'

'No, I'm not. I'm still Sue McCain, midwife.'

She checked her watch. Max insisted on exact timing. She was ready. She walked to the stage and stood in the wings. The band waved to her cheerfully. 'Don't say break a leg,' she told them. 'And Geordie says never say it to him again.' They laughed and she felt all right.

Max gave her a quick nod and walked out to the front of the stage. 'Ladies and gentlemen, we're very happy to see you. But this is not a performance, it's a dress rehearsal. Some things may be repeated, cut short, altered, and it may spoil the flow. This is for our benefit so we can put on a good show. But, still— enjoy.'

Behind the curtain the band started to play the soft introduction to her first number, the one she had got right eventually the night before—'You Left Me'. Too late now for second thoughts or panic. The curtain came up. She walked out to considerable applause, stood at the microphone and bowed. The applause didn't stop, but the band knew what to do and played the introduction again. And this time, 'I thought I had you but then you were gone. I thought I had love but then there was none…'

She was singing again. It was easy. In fact, it was great.

'Good, pretty good,' Max said a few minutes later. 'The timing was right, even with two encores. In fact, if you've got one, I'd like you to prepare another encore. Manage that?'

'No problem,' Sue said. 'We can use "The Last Goodnight". Remember it, lads?'

The band nodded. 'We'll run through it now if you like,' Griff said.

'Let's get it right now,' Max said. 'Better than tomorrow.'

There were other things that took them well into the evening. Max was a perfectionist and even though they'd had the dress rehearsal there were still changes he wanted to make. But finally even he was satisfied. 'It's good to work with you again Silver,' Stevie said. 'We're enjoying ourselves.'

'I'd forgotten how much fun it can be,' she said. 'I'll be round for a drink in a few minutes.'

Now she had finally finished work she had tried to phone Dan again. His mobile phone was switched off, and the hospital said he had left for the day. Feeling rather dispirited, she shared a taxi back to the hotel with the band. It was almost second nature to direct the driver round to a side entrance. But when they walked past the front desk the clerk said, 'Excuse me, Miss McCain. There's a man waiting to see you. He says he's your boss.'

She turned, and there was Dan in one of the foyer chairs. She ran over to hug him.

'Dan. It's so good to see you.' She realised she was with a group. 'You know the band, don't you?'

Of course he did. After greeting him cheerfully, Malcolm said, 'We've had a good afternoon and now we're going to have a drink. Care to join us?'

'No, he doesn't,' Sue said. 'He's coming up just to have a drink with me. See you all in the morning.' She took Dan's arm and led him to the lift. 'I've spent all day with other people,' she said. 'Now I want you just to myself. You have got time, haven't you, Dan?' she asked anxiously. 'I know you're busy but...'

He smiled. 'I'm on call at ten, in...' he looked at his watch '...about half an hour. I'll switch my mobile on then, but we shouldn't be disturbed.'

'I hope not. We haven't had any real time to ourselves for...a long time.' She led him down the thickly carpeted corridor to the door of her suite.

'There should be a bottle of white wine cooling in the fridge,' she told him, pointing to the ornate drinks cabinet. 'Give me a big kiss, then I'm going to have a shower—no, not a shower, a bath. You can bring us a drink and you can talk to me.'

She held out her arms for him to hug her. Then she looked apprehensive. He hadn't moved. 'What's the matter, Dan? Don't you want to kiss me?'

'You know I do! I'm just having a bit of difficulty coping with all this.' He waved his arm to indicate the ornate gold furniture, the draped and swagged curtains, the overly thick rugs. 'I'm not as happy here as I was in your house—in your garden.'

'Neither am I,' she said quickly. 'This isn't the life I want or like—it's just convenient. It's only for four days, Dan. I'm still Sue McCain—not Silver.'

Now he did kiss her. And she wanted him to continue—but they had all night. 'I'm going to get undressed and into the bath,' she told him. 'You uncork the wine.'

After undressing, she ran a full bath, poured in the expensive hotel foam and climbed in with an expression of bliss. 'Where's my wine?' she called. 'I've had a hard day.' He came in carrying two glasses, and sat in the cane chair by her bath. She took a glass and sipped. 'Look,' she said, 'we have...not problems but things we have to sort out. We can do it if we love each other. But everything has to go on hold for the next four days. Is that all right?'

'That's fine,' he said, 'even if you do sound like Max. Don't forget, I keep on reminding myself that you're doing this largely for me. But I'll be glad to see Midwife McCain again.'

'And I'll be glad to be her. Look, Dan, you've brought your mobile. Can you stay the night? Please?'

He grinned, and her heart lifted. He had been unusually solemn so far. 'You're asking me if I'll stay? I'll do more than that. Move over.'

His jacket and shirt were torn off and thrown out of the bathroom door. 'Ooh,' she squeaked, 'there's a naked man in my bathroom.'

'And in your bath,' he added, and climbed in with her. Well, it was a ludicrously big bath.

He kissed her, wet and soapy as she was. She

reached for the soap and rubbed her hands over his chest and shoulders. 'Why, you're all tensed up,' she said. 'Your muscles are all hard.'

'Quite,' he said, and she blushed.

After a while they just lay there. She could feel his toes rubbing the side of her arm. The tensions of the day had disappeared. 'This is fun,' she said. 'I wouldn't want to do it every day, but just now and again is fun.'

'I agree. Tomorrow I'll have to give myself a good going over with medical soap to get rid of this very expensive smell. But tonight I am enjoying myself.'

'I'm glad you came,' she said as he leaned forward. 'I was too tired to wash myself—nice to have it done for me. Dan! You've washed that bit four times already.'

'Sorry,' he said unrepentantly. 'My hands seem to have a mind of their own.'

It was very relaxing. Then she thought of something and frowned. 'I'm glad you came,' she said, 'I've got something to tell you—or ask you, if you like. You know Max has arranged a press conference tomorrow morning? Well, I've done them before, but there's...'

They both heard it. Out in her bedroom his mobile rang. He looked at her sadly, then climbed out of the bath, wrapped a towel round himself and stooped for the phone.

Equally sadly she listened to his conversation. 'Yes, Freddy... She what? No, get a theatre and an anaesthetist. I'm on my way.'

He was pulling on his shirt over his still damp body. When he was half-dressed he came to her and bent to kiss her through the foam. 'Listen, I doubt I'll be back. You know how it is.'

'Yes, I know how it is. I'm a midwife, remember. Bye, sweetheart.' And he was gone. She sighed, and took her last mouthful of white wine. It wasn't the same without someone to share it with.

Before she left next morning she phoned Geordie, who wished her good luck. Then she phoned the hospital and learned that Dan had been operating till the small hours. She decided not to phone and wake him. Now, just for the next four days, she was Sue McCain no more. She was Silver McCain again.

The first hurdle was the press conference. She knew through past experience that the best thing was to give them what they wanted. It was no good trying to hide. Max had arranged for them to come to the theatre. He had wanted to get alcohol for them, but she had vetoed it. 'Tea or coffee only,' she had instructed. 'I've suffered before when that lot have been drunk.'

She dressed in her full silver outfit and started by reading a short prepared statement. Flashlights twinkled in front of her as she carefully went through it. She had decided on a change in career, hadn't ever intended to sing again, this occasion was for charity only. An old friend, Geordie Summers, had persuaded her because he'd had an accident.

Then there were the questions. No, there was no way she would take up singing again full time. Even if this time was a success. Perhaps she would sing for charity, but no more than a couple of times a year. She had given it up because she didn't enjoy it any more. Her new career was that of a midwife. 'Can we see you in your uniform?' a sharp-faced female journalist asked. 'Only if your waters have broken and you're feeling contractions,' Sue answered cheerfully. She got a laugh—obviously the lady wasn't popular.

The questions became more personal. She remembered the golden rule—never lose your temper. 'Your husband was killed and your baby died just before you left the stage. Did that have anything to do with you giving up?' She gave a short answer. 'Possibly.'

Then the question came that she was expecting and dreading. 'Is there a man in your life now? Is there a gorgeous doctor somewhere ready to marry you?'

This was the question she had meant to warn Dan about, and had never had time. She knew that if she mentioned his name, for a few days his life would be made a misery. The press would scent a story. Keeping a straight face, she said, 'Certainly not. I have many good friends, but no special one. And I don't expect to find a gorgeous doctor. I'm happy in my work.'

She only just managed to hide her dismay at what she had had to say. At the back of the crowd she suddenly saw Dan. And he didn't look too happy at all.

She wanted to go and speak to him, but the reporters still gathered round her, seeking a personal quote to give them good copy. Only after another half-hour did she manage to escape, and by then Dan had gone.

His mobile was turned off and the hospital said that he was at work. The girl she spoke to knew who Sue was, and wished her luck. 'I'm coming to see you on Thursday,' she said. 'I'm really looking forward to it.' I wish I was, Sue thought, but said nothing wondering achingly if Dan would ever forgive her.

She went back to the hotel to sleep in the afternoon. That had always been her custom, as singing could be very tiring. Then, a couple of hours before she was due to go on, she drove down to the theatre and entered by the back way. This was it. The first time in over four years.

It was hard, but she had to remember she wasn't a star any more. Before, there had been people who'd protected her from her public, who'd let only a select few through the cordon. But many of these people were her friends—she had worked with them, would do so again. She signed autographs, promised pictures. Only one request did she always turn down—would she sing somewhere else? Each time she was asked this she said the same thing—that she had retired and she wouldn't sing again for at least six months.

Eventually she got to her dressing room, and called Stella to guard the door. Only Max—or Dan if he turned up—was to be allowed in. She had to get herself together. There were flowers in the dressing room—from Max, from Geordie, from Jane and Megan and from others. There was nothing from Dan. Well, perhaps he didn't know the custom of sending flowers for a first night.

She felt like crying. It wasn't just first-night nerves. The last person she had spoken to had been a singer in the choir, a woman who'd had her husband and her six-month-old baby with her. The baby had beautiful, wispy, white hair. 'It's almost silver, isn't it?' the woman had said proudly. 'We call her Silver, although her name's Sylvia really.'

That had reminded Sue of the last time she had sung, in a large hall in London. She had been five months pregnant, and happy in her pregnancy. Then she had lost her baby. She had also lost her husband, but she had been pleased about that.

In the distance she could hear the sounds of the first

half of the programme. It seemed to be going well. Then it was time to put on her first dress, her make-up and wig. Max came in, looking sophisticated in his dinner jacket. 'It's not going too badly,' he said. 'For a half-amateur cast, it's not too bad at all.'

'I feel sick, Max.'

'Of course you do. Have a drink of water.' He passed her a glass. 'And here's something that has just arrived. I wish people would be on time.'

He gave her two tiny pots. Both held fuchsias. One was the darkest of reds, the other so white as to be almost silver. She recognised it at once—it was the one William had been propagating. There were two cards. One said, 'Love, William, Gladys, Alice, Mickey, Helen and Stephen.' The other said, 'All my love, Dan.'

'I don't feel sick any more,' she said. 'Let's get started.'

She stood in the wings, winked and waved at the band. Looking lonely at the front of the stage was her microphone, with a spotlight on it. The front-of-house lights went down, and the buzz of conversations grew quiet.

Max stepped through the curtains, and said, 'Ladies and gentleman—Silver McCain.' There was a storm of applause. She swallowed and took two breaths as the curtains drew back. There was that darkness, which had always seemed so perilous to her. But it was full of her friends.

The band started her introduction, she walked on stage, clasped her hands and bowed. The applause swelled and she had to wait until they were ready to hear her. The band played her introduction again and she began, 'I thought I had you but then you were gone. I thought I had love but then there was none.'

It went well, and after that there was no stopping her.

The programme had been carefully arranged—she had always been good at preparation. She moved from a slow love song to something more upbeat and comic. Then another slow song. Between the numbers she talked about her new career as a midwife, about the hospital charity they were working for. She didn't forget to thank Geordie and introduce the band. She finished the first half of her programme with a fast, hard-beating affirmation of the power of love.

The curtain came down and she skipped into the wings. She stripped off her outfit and was helped into the second dress by Stella. She dabbed cologne on her forehead. Max came up. For the first time ever she saw him enthusiastic. 'You're wonderful,' he said. 'Listen, they're lapping you up.'

She went back on stage for the rest of her act, and still had to do three encores. Then she came off, elated. She had forgotten what a high it was, forgotten the feeling of power that having an audience gave her, making them live with her own words. It felt so good!

She was congratulated by everyone backstage. There was the suggestion of a bit of a party, but Max said she wasn't to stay. She had just returned to singing after a long layoff, she wasn't to tire herself. One thing she did do was phone Geordie. He had made her promise that she'd let him know how it had gone. 'Not bad at all, Geordie,' she said.

'Don't try to kid an old trouper. I can tell by your voice. You knocked them into the aisles, didn't you?'

'Well, yes,' she said modestly.

Clutching her two precious fuchsias in her arms, she took a taxi back to the hotel. She told the hotel management that she would accept no calls, but kept her own mobile by her. And then she phoned Dan, who finally spoke to her.

'I couldn't make the show,' he said quietly, 'but I heard it went really well.'

She could hear the doubt and a faint anger in his voice. 'You heard what I said to the press about not having a man in my life,' she said. 'Dan, I said that to save you problems. I didn't mean it. That's what I was going to tell you yesterday, but you disappeared. You didn't want reporters chasing you, did you?'

'I suppose not,' he said slowly. 'I forget that you know this business backwards.'

'I'm remembering. And I don't like all I remember. Dan, would you like to come round?'

'I'd like to. But there are a couple of cases here I've got to keep my eye on. But I'm thinking of you.'

He rang off. She felt rather low, but decided to go to bed. She had work to do tomorrow evening. And Friday and Saturday. But after that her own life would come first!

Thursday and Friday both went well. On Friday she had to stay behind late because of the television crew. Dan had arranged to sell the rights to the show for a ridiculous sum, and she performed not only to an audience but also to a battery of TV cameras. But at the end of the show there were certain things they still hadn't got right so she had to stay behind and sing again. She was a professional so she did it. There was also a television interview. It went well. She talked about her work as a midwife.

Then it was Saturday, the final night. She had rehearsed another two songs so the show went on a little longer and she ended on top of the world. She knew how much she owed to all sorts of people, so she stayed behind for the party afterwards. It was good that everything was now over.

'Have you seen Dan?' she asked Max.

'I know he was here for your performance,' Max said, 'but apparently he was called back to the hospital.'

Well, he had seen her. The party was breaking up now. She refused an invitation to join the band back at their hotel and took a taxi to the hospital. On Monday night she would be back at work there. As a midwife. She needed to get back in touch with it. And the rest of her real life.

She found Dan in the doctors' room, writing up notes. Apparently he'd had to insert a Shirodkar suture, a nylon loop round the bottom of the cervix. Some mothers had cervical incompetence, a weak cervix that led them to abort spontaneously A Shirodkar suture held in the growing foetus. Doctors had told her that it was a satisfying operation to perform.

She opened the door quietly and watched him for a while, unnoticed. Then she said, 'Can I get you a coffee, doctor? I fancy one myself.'

He looked up and smiled at her low-key approach. 'What are you doing here?'

'I came to see my favourite man. My lover. You finish what you're doing and I'll get the coffee.'

A warm and loving light came into his eyes then, and all reserve fell away. 'All right, then.' He bent his head to his writing, the notes that were never to be left undone. Eventually it was finished and he pushed the file away.

'I watched your performance tonight,' he said. 'In fact, I've watched every night. But tonight was different. You came alive in that spotlight, you were a lover to all the audience. They felt it, so you must have done.'

'It's all just an illusion,' she said uneasily. 'I know that's how they feel, and I'd be lying if I said I didn't get a kick out of it. But it's all over now.'

'Do you want to go back to it? I know you said you didn't but, after watching you, how can you bear to give it up?'

'I can because I want to. My life is now the hospital and...' Her voice trailed away.

'And?' he asked.

'Thank you for the fuchsias,' she said. 'How did you know that they were just the thing to make me feel confident? And isn't the silver one the one William has just grown?'

'It is. He saw the show, by the way—the whole family did, and they thought you were wonderful. And William wanted you to have the flower. He wants to call it Silver McCain—he says it will sell a million with a name like that.'

'The flower will sell, not the name,' she told him. 'Dan why are we talking like this? I'm your lover!'

He stood and wrapped his arms round her. 'I wondered when I saw you this evening if I was going to lose you. I thought you might want a new life—or an old one.'

'Never,' she said. 'I want to be a midwife. More

than that, I want you…and a ready-made family. I love you all.'

He kissed her. 'In that case, you'd better join the family properly,' he said. 'Will you marry me, Sue?'

'I will, Dan,' she said. 'Oh, yes, I will.'

MILLS & BOON®

Makes any time special™

Mills & Boon publish 29 new titles every month. Select from...

Modern Romance™   Tender Romance™

Sensual Romance™

Medical Romance™   Historical Romance™

MAT2

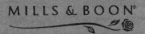

MILLS & BOON®

Medical Romance™

JUMPING TO CONCLUSIONS *by Judy Campbell*

Desperate for help in her practice, Dr Kathy
MacDowell is forced to accept Dr Will Curtis, despite
such bad feelings between their families. She soon
realises that not only is he a good doctor, he's also
deeply attractive…

FINGER ON THE PULSE *by Abigail Gordon*

Dr Leonie Marsden's first day in her new paediatric job
ends with some bad news about her own health.
Determined not to let down hospital manager, Adam
Lockhart, she soldiers on but soon the secret forms a
serious barrier between them…

THE MOST PRECIOUS GIFT *by Anne Herries*

Bachelor Doctors

Encountering old flame Megan Hastings had ignited past
feelings for Dr Philip Grant. It wasn't until Megan had to
face a serious illness that he realised this was the
woman he wanted.

On sale 1st September 2000

*Available at most branches of WH Smith, Tesco,
Martins, Borders, Easons, Volume One/James Thin
and most good paperback bookshops*

0008/03a

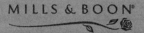

Medical Romance™

AN IRRESISTIBLE INVITATION by *Alison Roberts*

No. 1 of a Trilogy

When trainee GP Sophie Bennett began work at St David's Medical Centre, her attraction to her supervisor, Dr Oliver Spencer, was instantaneous. But he's made it clear he's not looking for commitment and she has a secret to hide...

THE TIME IS NOW by *Gill Sanderson*

No. 2 of a Trilogy

Anaesthetist David Kershaw was quite beautiful yet he took no notice of his looks or the impact they had on the women around him. Theatre Sister Jane Cabot realised it was entirely her own fault if she had preconceived ideas about him but could she change her mind?

FOR BEN'S SAKE by *Jennifer Taylor*

Dalverston General Hospital

When Sister Claire Shepherd discovers that the new locum A&E doctor is none other than Sean Fitzgerald, her heart misses a beat. Although she'd acted with the best of intentions, how could Claire confess to him that her son Ben was also his own?

On sale 1st September 2000

0008/03b

FREE!

4 Books
and a surprise gift!

We would like to take this opportunity to thank you for reading this Mills & Boon® book by offering you the chance to take FOUR more specially selected titles from the Medical Romance™ series absolutely FREE! We're also making this offer to introduce you to the benefits of the Reader Service™—

- ★ FREE home delivery
- ★ FREE gifts and competitions
- ★ FREE monthly Newsletter
- ★ Books available before they're in the shops
- ★ Exclusive Reader Service discounts

Accepting these FREE books and gift places you under no obligation to buy; you may cancel at any time, even after receiving your free shipment. Simply complete your details below and return the entire page to the address below. *You don't even need a stamp!*

YES! Please send me 4 free Medical Romance books and a surprise gift. I understand that unless you hear from me, I will receive 6 superb new titles every month for just £2.40 each, postage and packing free. I am under no obligation to purchase any books and may cancel my subscription at any time. The free books and gift will be mine to keep in any case.

MOZEB

Ms/Mrs/Miss/Mr ....Initials.................................
BLOCK CAPITALS PLEASE

Surname...

Address...

....

....Postcode ....

Send this whole page to:
UK: The Reader Service, FREEPOST CN81, Croydon, CR9 3WZ
EIRE: The Reader Service, PO Box 4546, Kilcock, County Kildare (stamp required)